P9-ASC-296

HARVEST IN TRANSLATION

Missing Pieces

Missing Pieces

stories by

Stanislaw Benski

translated by Walter Arndt

A Harvest/HBJ Book
A Helen and Kurt Wolff Book
Harcourt Brace Jovanovich, Publishers
San Diego New York London

Library of Congress Cataloging-in-Publication Data
Benski, Stanisław, 1922–1988
Missing pieces: stories/by Stanisław Benski ; translated by Walter Arndt.—1st ed.
p. cm.
"A Helen and Kurt Wolff book."
ISBN 0-15-160585-8
ISBN 0-15-660798-0 (pbk.)
1. Holocaust survivors—Poland—Fiction.
2. Benski, Stanisław, 1922–1988
—Translations, English. I. Title.
PG7161.E52A23 1989
891.8′537—dc20 89-28133

Printed in the United States of America

First Harvest/HBJ edition 1992

A B C D E

HBJ

Contents

Missing Pieces

The Tzaddik's Grandson

Chaim always got up at sunrise. He ate little. Bread, an egg, a potato, sometimes a little herring. He wore a black caftan which dated back to prewar times, trousers of the same vintage, and tzitzis or, as the attendant Marysia called them, a pony fringe. For prayer, Chaim put on a tallis, which she called a scarf, and also the tefillin on his head and hand, which she called little prayer boxes.

"He is a saint," Marysia once said. "Yesterday he looked at me, and my toothache stopped at once."

One Sunday, she asked him to bless her little Kamilka, who had had a high fever for a week and a dry cough. Chaim gazed at Marysia, nodded, and the next morning Kamilka was well. Some even maintained he was a tzaddik. But there were a few who did not believe Marysia. The attendant Hanka, for example, or Julka the laundress, or Walek the janitor, who had fallen out with Marysia when she told him his nose was red from drinking too much vodka.

Chaim permitted no one but Marysia to clean his room.

The physician who kept Chaim's case history had written: "Antisocial. No relatives." And in parentheses: "Schizophrenia?"

Chaim showed no interest whatever in his medical condition. Once, during Purim, he got diarrhea, but recovered after two days. The medicine which the nurse gave him he placed in the corridor outside his door.

Just before Passover, six taxis pulled up in front of the home. From the first emerged Nachum. He looked up and down the street and raised his right hand. Immediately, from the remaining taxis, with measured dignity, Jews got out, Jews dressed in long black caftans, collars, fur caps, white stockings, and black patent leather slippers. Two women emerged from the last taxi, a young one who held a baby wrapped in black cloth and an older one dressed in black. The older woman entered the building first, the younger one followed, and the men came last.

"What can I do for you, ladies, gentlemen?" asked the concierge, Helena, taken aback.

"We have come from New York and wish to see Chaim, who lives here with you," said one of the visitors.

Nachum started up the stairs, but the concierge said: "Nachum, surely you know that one can't have so many visitors at once."

Nachum stopped.

"And as I look at you, ladies, gentlemen, you are so strangely dressed . . . Aren't they, Nachum?" she went on. "Who knows what the people here will think. . . . I, for one, never saw such outfits before. Anyway, visits to patients are limited to one person at a time. At most, two or three."

"My dear woman," the older lady said, "it took us three days by airplane to get here. We want to see Chaim."

"Mrs. Helena," Nachum said to the concierge in a loud voice, "you know that Chaim won't see anyone, but if you tell him that the wife of a God-fearing Jew has arrived, a Jew who is from the same shtetl as Chaim, he will . . ."

"Excuse me," said an old man with a long white beard, "but she is in fact the widow of a great rabbi, a wonder-working tzaddik."

"Shh!" whispered Nachum. "People will guess that Jews from America have come to visit the tzaddik's grave."

"We are Polish Jews," the wonder-working tzaddik's widow said to Nachum, "and there is no reason to conceal that we have come to visit my husband's grave, and that we also want to see Reb Chaim."

"He won't see you," the concierge declared. "He won't even talk to me. Marysia isn't here. She's the only one who can go into his room. The only one he listens to. Come, Nachum."

On the staircase appeared Feivel and, behind him, Rose. They were curious about the newcomers. Feivel turned back but reappeared after a while with several other pensioners. There was blind Moses, and Sarah, who was not only blind but deaf, too, and Samuel, who hobbled on legs twisted by Little's disease, and old Julius, and David, who was even older.

"People to see our Chaim," Nachum announced, going up the stairs. "They have come from a great distance!"

"What?" asked Julius, who was hard of hearing.

"You can see that they have come from a great distance," said Samuel. "But Chaim won't see anyone."

"Just what I told them," the concierge said. "They'll have to wait for Marysia."

"Rebbetzin," Nachum addressed the tzaddik's widow, "you'll have to wait for Marysia."

"Send for this Marysia, then," demanded the tzaddik's widow. "We have dollars, we'll pay for it."

"She lives outside Warsaw, in the country," said the concierge.

"It doesn't matter," snapped the woman, and took some green bills out of her handbag.

"Chaim won't see anyone," said Samuel.

After a moment of indecision, the tzaddik's widow put the bills back into her handbag and said, "I am going up. Me he will see. Lead the way, Nachum!"

The concierge opened the elevator door, and Nachum rode up to the third floor with the tzaddik's widow. The rest of the visitors seated themselves in the various chairs in the lobby and waited.

A group of pensioners continued to stand on the mezzanine landing and watched the bearded Jews who had come from America. Feivel was the first to venture down.

"You're Jewish?" he asked.

"That should be obvious," replied a man who sat by the window.

"Rich?"

"No."

"You're poor?"

"No."

"Then what are you?"

"Pious, honest."

"Not everyone who is honest is pious," observed Feivel. "I am honest, but not a believer."

"Then you are not a Jew," said the oldest of the visitors.

"I *am* a Jew," said Feivel, angry. "I lived through the Warsaw ghetto. Did you live through the Warsaw ghetto?"

They were silent.

Feivel approached the man sitting by the window. "On Yom Kippur they killed my wife! And on Passover, they burned my little Avrum to death! How can I be a believer?"

Rose pulled Feivel aside. "Don't, you mustn't," she whispered. "They don't understand."

"Feivel," said the concierge, "you are not supposed to excite yourself. Do you remember what happened on Thursday? Do you? Calm down, or I'll have to ring for the nurse."

"He'll be quiet," said Rose. "I'll stay with him, please don't ring, Mrs. Helena. He won't shout."

David, Julius, and Samuel came down the stairs and stood near Feivel.

"What's the trouble?" asked Samuel.

"They say I'm not a Jew," said Feivel. "Maybe you can tell them . . ."

The oldest of the visitors rose and went up to Samuel.

"We have collected a few dollars for you."

"We don't need your money," said Feivel, still indignant.

"We can use it!" Samuel shouted. "We'll buy oranges for the people on the fourth floor."

"Who are the people on the fourth floor?" asked the visitor.

"Paralytics and the terminally ill," Julius explained. "But you shouldn't worry, they are taken good care of."

"Oranges is a good idea," Samuel said. "They have no families, those people, no relatives. Oranges is a good idea."

"What child is this?" asked David, pointing at the baby which the young woman was now trying to nurse.

"A sick child, a very sick child," said the old man, frowning, "the tzaddik's grandson. We are here because of him."

"What do you mean, because of him?" asked Rose, going up to the young mother.

"At the tzaddik's grave we will ask for mercy for this child. The tzaddik will heal his grandson."

"May he give him much health and happiness," said Rose quietly. "I had three children. Three wonderful boys. By now I could have had grandchildren."

"I too could have had grandchildren," said Feivel.

"Let me hold the little one a while," Rose begged.

"Here," said the mother, handing her the little bundle. "But be careful, don't let go."

Rose walked with the baby in the hall and into the adjoining dining room, where the attendants were eating.

"Got yourself a kid?" Józia laughed and came over to Rose.

"He isn't mine, he's a sacred child, a tzaddik's grandson. You don't know, of course, what a tzaddik is. There was one here before the War. There aren't any tzaddiks now. They all died off."

"And did *you* ever see one?" Józia asked, caressing with the fingers of her broad hand the tiny head of the infant, who began to cry.

"Don't fret, little one." Rose moved the child from her right arm to her left. "Yes, I have seen tzaddiks. I was at the court of the Kozienicki tzaddik and of the tzaddik from Mount

Calvary. My father took me to those places. He supplied them with cloth for caftans and suits. My father was a hat maker by trade, but that's a long time ago. . . . I remember the Hasidim in Kozienice dancing the *mayufes*. The yarmulkes sailed off their heads, their *peyis* fluttered over their ears, and the tails of their caftans spun in the air as they sang and danced. It was *Simches Toyre*, but that was twenty years ago."

The tzaddik's grandson cried louder, and neither Józia's fingers nor Rose's whispers of "Hush, little one" helped. The mother, hearing her baby cry, came running.

"He's crying! Wonderful!" she exclaimed.

"I don't understand," said Józia, astonished.

"He hasn't cried, he has been silent since birth. The doctors did not think he would survive our journey. And here he is, crying . . . wonderful! My child is crying!"

"You're young and you speak Polish," said Józia. "I thought only old people still remembered the language."

"We live on Twelfth Street where everybody speaks Polish."

The American visitors crowded around the mother and child. The infant cried with a passion. Then Rose announced triumphantly:

"He wetted himself, all over!"

The men returned to their former places, while the women changed the tzaddik's grandson's diaper.

The elevator opened, and out came the tzaddik's widow, then Nachum, then Chaim. The visitors stood up.

"Has Chaim really come out of his little room?" said Feivel in awe.

"Let him stand against the wall," said the man by the window. "Let's take his picture."

The visitors all had cameras, and they formed a row facing Chaim.

"They look like a firing squad," remarked Feivel, and turned away.

Chaim stood, bewildered by the flashes and the unfamiliar room, then turned around and pattered back toward the open elevator door. He paused, turned left, and resolutely started up the stairs.

"Reb Chaim," called Nachum, "Reb Chaim! We had an agreement, you know. You promised to talk to our visitors here. We had an agreement!"

But Chaim slowly climbed up and in another moment disappeared around the bend of the staircase.

Colored Drawings

There were nine of them: Haskiel, Abram, Boruch, Julian, Chaim, Nachum, Feivel, Samuel, and Elias.

"What are we waiting for?" asked Nachum, always impatient.

"We are waiting for the tenth," said Samuel matter-of-factly.

"One, two, three, four, five, six, seven, eight, and myself is nine," Feivel counted.

"You can count, you're a genius," said Samuel.

"We can't pray, we don't have a minyan, we might as well go," Julian said, and got up from his chair.

"Let's wait," said blind Abram quietly. "Someone may come."

Julian walked over to the window and opened it wide, but closed it again quickly. It was snowing out there, and the wind blew straight in one's eyes. He sat down again at the table, where the prayer books lay.

"We should have asked them to leave us at least one Jew," said Feivel.

"I don't understand," said Boruch.

"You never understand." Feivel laughed. "Didn't a whole group of American Jews visit us a few weeks ago and ask us what we needed? . . . They went to a tzaddik's grave to ask mercy for his little grandson. Yes, that was a sick child. . . . And when they asked us what we needed, we should have asked them to leave us one American Jew, to make a minyan. With his dollars that person could have rented a decent room, and feeding him would have been no problem. He could have a kosher breakfast here cheap, and kosher lunches, and kosher suppers. And for *Shabbos,* Malke could make him chicken. I don't know if you remember, but one of those Americans was a young redheaded bachelor. He told me he lived in the Bronx, while here he would live in the very center of Warsaw. His late mother lived right here on Gęsia Street, and his father was born in Sochaczew. . . ."

"What's more," threw in Julian, "we could have married him off, for example to Rivka. Oh, I know, you'll say she's crippled, with only one leg and the left one at that, and that she's poor. But she comes from a good family. We should definitely find her a husband. Haskiel is young, but she doesn't want him, because Haskiel, as you can see, has a small hump. Some girls like hunchbacks, others look only at straight boys. . . . Our Rivka is one of those."

"I don't want her either!" said Haskiel, angry. "Rivka's not my type."

"Haskiel likes them tall and hefty. The kind that weigh over two hundred pounds on the hoof." Julian laughed and leaned back so far that he nearly fell from his chair.

"We were supposed to say kaddish," admonished Samuel.

"Do Jews have to be sad all the time? Do we always have to talk misfortune?" asked Nachum. "Let's give our Rivka a few smiles, a little hope. Let's find her a husband. She should leave the home and live on her own. The girl cooks, launders, helps in the kitchen, feeds the sick."

"She embroiders, she draws," added Julian.

"She sings," said Haskiel.

"She has a pretty voice," said Chaim.

Elias remembered walking with Rivka on the bank of the Vistula. They had walked slowly and not talked much at first. Every now and then, Rivka stopped to pick up a stone and throw it into the water. It was a hot day, and on the other side of the river you could see a great number of men, women, and children lying in the sand or strolling along the bank. Their bodies, various shades of brown, were in bathing suits, and the caps, hoods, and kerchiefs on their heads were red, white, blue, green. Here and there, enormous beach umbrellas stuck out, and on the sand and grassy slopes lay bright blankets, sheets, towels, all making a lively, continually changing picture that shimmered with color. You could hear a hum of voices, calls, shouts, and music from radios. Beyond the beach rose four high-rise buildings like slender white boxes. They were the new apartment buildings built in the Praga district.

Elias sometimes thought of moving there, to the top floor. From his window he would be able to see Gnojna Góra, Starówka, the New City, the Vistula.

"You're all dressed up today," Elias said, regarding Rivka. "A red dress with white polka dots, a pretty kerchief around the neck . . ."

Rivka laughed, bent down, took a large pebble, and pitched it hard into the water. There was a loud splash as the stone vanished.

Elias took a smaller flat pebble and flung it in the same direction. It skipped on the surface once, twice, three times before it sank. Rivka clapped.

"Wonderful, Eli. Where did you learn that?"

"From a friend."

She looked at him with surprise. "You have a friend? I thought you were alone."

"I am, but a man helped me once."

"Helped you?"

"He saved my life. A human being, a mensch. But your life was saved, too. They hid you?"

"My mother hid me."

"Your mother?" Elias asked in surprise.

"My second mother," Rivka corrected herself. "I loved her, but the Lord took her away, and I am alone again. Mrs. Wojciechowski was a railroad man's widow. On the tracks she found a little crippled Jewish girl who jumped from a train. A train that was going to the ovens of Treblinka . . . Mrs. Wojciechowski was childless, so the Lord sent her a little girl, and she took her in as her own. The Lord works in mysterious ways."

"He does," Elias agreed. After a silence he added, "But you are still young and pretty."

"Yes, and my dowry is my crutch." She held out the wooden crutch, standing on her one leg and looking straight into Elias's eyes.

"Careful!" he said, and went to put an arm around her.

But Rivka smiled and jumped aside, not falling, still standing on her one leg.

"You see how I can handle myself? You see? And my arms are strong." She held out her arms. "Look at them, feel them!"

Elias caught the girl's hands in his, but again Rivka pulled away with a few one-legged hops, until she reached a nearby bench and sat down. Elias walked over to her.

"Yes, you are strong. You'll do all right. . . ."

Rivka turned away. "Eli, I wanted to kiss you. You're a good man, Eli. I'm ashamed."

"People need people," sighed Elias. "Sometimes for a short while, sometimes for one day or night, sometimes for a whole lifetime."

Rivka spoke as though to herself. "You won't understand, but I have dreams, premonitions. And something to show you—but not a word to anyone. Swear!"

"I swear!"

Out of her handbag she took two small scrolls of paper and unrolled one of them. Elias saw a drawing, in color, of a child. The child had big green eyes, a bright blonde shock of hair, and held a yellow rose in one little fist. In the other it held what looked like a lead soldier without a head. The soldier wore a black swastika on his chest. Over the child hovered a yellow bird. Rivka laid the scroll on the bench, unrolled the second, and gave it to Elias.

Elias saw a sky-blue embankment on which stood a closed freight car ringed by garlands of flowers. There were sunflowers, roses, poppies, pansies, and tulips, and among the flowers were green music notes, red bows, and cockades, dots, and sashes. The railroad car, beige with blue stripes, had a black chimney from which came whorls of smoke. Beside the car stood a hazy little figure, a woman.

"And who is this?" asked Elias, pointing to the woman.

"My second mother."

"You draw well. You'll be a famous painter."

"Oh, don't talk like that. . . . Or I won't show you any more."

He smiled and sat down beside her.

"I mean it. They're very good," he said, returning the scroll to her with a smile.

"You know, Eli . . . I wish that everything that happened hadn't happened. Tell me that everything Rivka went through is a lie, a fantasy, a fairy tale made up by an evil sorcerer, by Baba Yaga, the witch who flies on a broom. Say it, Eli . . . Say that I made it all up, please, Eli."

"I can't . . ."

"Please!"

"All right, then, you made it all up. There was no War, no Ghetto, no Treblinka. . . . There is a street, and on the street there is a house, a small house, and in the house lives a little girl with her parents. The little girl is pretty . . . no, beautiful, and happy. She studies arithmetic and Polish and geography and drawing, and then later she becomes a great painter, famous all over the world, and marries a God-fearing Jew, and they have children, and then their children marry and have children, and all this happens in the same little town, which has a synagogue, and a rabbi, and a pharmacist, and a notary, and a tavern and a tiny hotel, and to the nearest railroad station it's ten kilometers. . . ."

"Seven," Rivka said, but Elias went on: "Our painter's house stands on a wide street. At noon, in summer, when the sun is hot and the street is deserted, dogs lie stretched out, and on a wall or window ledge a cat sleeps. Before evening the street begins to fill. After working in the fields all day, or in the workshops and little stores, the men sit in front of their houses, some on benches and chairs, some on empty barrels and boxes. The elderly and sick are brought outside and given the best seats, and clean cushions are put under their heads. Everyone talks.

"The men, stroking their beards, talk politics, business, complain a little, sigh a little, but laugh a lot. The women, adjusting their *sheitels,* gossip or exchange advice on cooking and cleaning, baking and laundering. The girls and boys do what they usually do: the youngest play games, chase each other, shout, jump in the sand, while the older ones read books under a tree in the little garden, or tease each other. The young girls provoke the boys, but sometimes a boy gets even with a sharp-tongued girl by pulling her pigtails, but he doesn't pull too hard, just enough.

"A horse and wagon pass by, raising a cloud of dust behind it, which blocks the view for a moment, and you can hear the squeals of the small children and the women's scolding. After that, everyone calms down and returns to the twilight conversation. They drink bread kvass, lemonade, sour milk with sugar, camomile tea, or tea with jam in it. . . .

"The little town also has a market, and in this market the booths are arranged in a half-circle. In the first booth, shoes and slippers are sold for men, women, and children; in the second, harnesses for horses, ropes, chains, and buckets; in the third, plates, spoons, teapots, and dishes; in the fourth, buttons, bows, ribbon, paper flowers, buckles, and red summer dresses with white polka dots. . . ."

"You told it well," Rivka said, and raised her hand as if to touch Elias's shoulder, but withdrew it at once.

"And now we're in Warsaw," said Elias. "It's the beginning of summer, people are sunbathing. The children are out of school and having fun in the mountains, at the seaside, in meadows and woods. A train from Paris pulls into Gdańsk Station, the shops sell fresh rolls and butter, and Rivka sits with Elias on a bench by the Vistula."

He paused. Rivka lifted her head. He noticed a tiny white blossom at the neck of her dress, a brooch in the shape of a daisy. And in the girl's ears were earrings, also in the shape of a daisy, only smaller. Once, a very long time ago, when Grandmother Pesia was taking him to the Seder, they stopped at Isaac's booth, and Grandmother Pesia bought a brooch like that. Elias remembered very clearly Grandmother bargaining with Isaac, as if the brooch were pure gold.

"Go on," said Rivka.

But Elias was silent. He half-closed his eyes and sat in thought, until he heard the girl singing. She sang very softly. Elias knew that the song was for him. He didn't catch all the words, because it was more a crooning than a song. Yet from time to time he caught a word, a phrase: "Dancing, you and I . . . on a sunny road . . ."

When he opened his eyes, Rivka was gone. He looked around, saw her walking in the direction of Gnojna Góra, and a doubt assailed him. Had he really been sitting with her, had they really talked, had she really sung him a song about dancing on a sunny road?

Rivka, meanwhile, walked rapidly away, throwing her crutch forward, shifting her body to the left, to the right, as she passed the strolling people. Her red dress played hide-and-seek in the crowd.

Elias followed her at a certain distance, then caught up with her just before she reached the steps.

"I'll buy you an ice cream," he said.

"I accept," she said, and practically skipped up the steps, still humming her song.

So Elias mused as he sat at the table with the prayer books, waiting with the others for a tenth Jew.

The Round

Julian had taken care of Leizor for thirteen years. He had treated him like a natural son: punished him, praised him, woke him up in the morning, made him wash his neck and ears, made him swallow pills, laundered his socks, and shaved him. They would go out together—to shop, to stroll, to the synagogue. Leizor always walked ahead, and old Julian could not keep up.

"Don't rush," Julian scolded. "You'll get there! Watch out for cars. If a car hits you, you'll end up like Simche, who was run over by a truck on his way to buy soda water. Watch where you're going, nudnik, you're thirty years old."

Leizor nodded and walked ahead as before.

Julian's workday began with the Round. First he went into room 16 on the second floor, which was occupied by the two Miss Marys, and asked in his big, hoarse baritone:

"What will you have, Miss Mary, and you, Miss Mary, what will you have?"

"The paper for me, and half a kilo of apples," the elder Miss Mary answered, as always.

"Soda water," said the younger Miss Mary.

Then Julian would knock at the doors of several rooms on the third floor and a few on the fourth, and take more orders.

On Fridays he called on the Deremans, who were blind. It happened that on this particular Friday he started with them.

"Today is Friday, the Lord be praised," said Julian. "Should I buy a challah, a chicken, a box of candles?"

"Yes," answered Mr. Dereman, as he always did. "Buy the chicken, take it to the *shochet,* and then Malka will clean and cook it. Everything must be kosher. But today I can't make soup, I don't have the strength. My head aches."

"We'll still need parsley and carrots," called Malka, who was busy in the corridor and every now and then put her head into the Deremans' room.

"What? Who?" Sarah Dereman, blind and deaf, asked in a very loud voice.

"Julian is here to take our order for *Shabbos*!" Dereman shouted into his wife's ear. "He is buying a challah, a chicken, and candles!"

"Ah, a challah for *Shabbos*! A chicken for soup! And *Shabbos* candles! Julian is so kind. May the Lord bless him and give him ever so much health and happiness."

From the Deremans Julian went straight to Masha.

"So what will it be for you? Today is Friday."

"On Fridays I have a quarter kilo of hard candy," Masha said.

"Raspberry, lemon, or mint?"

"Raspberry," Masha decided.

The six-person suite took Julian longer. Here the orders were complicated. Rose, for instance, asked for six apples, but they mustn't weigh over a kilo in all. Anna wanted a bar of cream-filled chocolate, but the cream had to be coffee-flavored. Chaya insisted on a braided challah, while Rivka asked for cream rolls topped with poppy seeds. It was just such a roll that her husband, Abram, baked before the War, and Rivka took every opportunity to tell people how he made them in their bakery, and how in that same bakery a German officer killed him, and how her Abram ended up lying on the table on which with his own hands he had made such rolls.

"The table was white, white as snow with the flour," Rivka said, "and Abram's face was just as white, like the best-grade wheat flour."

"That's all I ever hear from you!" Julian grumbled. "Always thinking back how things used to be, as if you were an aristocrat, a Rothschild, but now what you spend is only a few lousy zlotys, not thousands, as you used to. And it all falls on my poor gray head . . ."

Julian concluded his round by dropping in on the attorney, Mr. Bodol.

"Respects to you, sir," he saluted him. "How's the old health? Did you sleep well?"

"Have a seat," the attorney said.

Julian sat in the armchair. The attorney adjusted the pillow under his back, narrowed his eyes, and listened.

"Dvoira had an attack last night," reported Julian. "Pain in the gall bladder area. The nurse gave her two injections, one at one, the other at six in the morning. Fredek had another epileptic fit and, as usual, screamed too loudly. . . ."

"Yes, I heard him," confirmed the attorney.

"Rose complains about her heart," Julian resumed, "and the lady doctor was late for lunch yesterday and found the stuffed dumplings cold. The bookkeeper spent two hours standing in line for payroll money. The waitress Kasia got a doctor's statement that she was out with a sore throat or else pregnant. The janitor and the furnace man unloaded a shipment of flour and sugar and got it done in half an hour. Leizor turned thirty yesterday and says he has pains in his side. It's probably his liver. The elder Miss Mary must be feeling better, because she has finally started cursing America again. And you, sir, are still smoking those stinking cigarettes." Julian, his report finished, reached for the empty seltzer syphon that stood on the table.

"Wait," said Mr. Bodol. "You know, Julian, I keep thinking about . . . that business. I can't seem to get it out of my head. . . ."

"You mustn't let it get you down. You have everything you want now. A clean bed, a roof over your head, central heating, medicine, food—and a syphon of seltzer every day, which I buy for you."

"But the question of what I am . . ."

"What question? Why should there be a question? You torment yourself, yet the War is over, the Occupation is over. You should read—newspapers, books—and listen to the radio, and talk to intelligent people, like Julian in Number Twelve."

"Julian . . ." The attorney fell back against his pillow. "I don't know . . . if what I did was right."

Julian scratched his head. "Perhaps it was, perhaps it wasn't."

"You see? You too have doubts."

Julian got up and went to the window. For a while he watched two bickering sparrows on the balcony railing, then turned back. "What you did, you had to do."

"She saved my life." The attorney sat up again. "Every day, she saved my life. She got me out of the Ghetto. The Gestapo lived in the apartment below us. Later, a son was born, my son. He had to be baptized. I too . . ."

"Let me tell you something," Julian said. "What went on in those times, nobody—that is, the young generation—will ever understand. And the people who lived elsewhere then, over the mountains, over the seas, they haven't the right to judge us. You mustn't torment yourself, Mr. Bodol, about the past. The important things now are good digestion, regularity, a good bladder, a good maid, good nurses and doctors, and intelligent Julian in Number Twelve on the second floor."

"I will make a note of our conversation today." The attorney drew a thick notebook from under his pillow.

"What's that?" asked Julian, intrigued.

"I write things down."

"Is there a lot of written stuff?"

"The book is almost half full. . . . It gives me relief. I record what we say, your wisdom."

"I have no wisdom. I have vices. I drink too much. I used to be a waiter at the Savoy Restaurant, so I drank like a waiter. It stayed with me . . . an occupational hazard. When I feel a bad spell coming, I take phenactyl, but sometimes I'm too late. The feeling is like missing a train, like being left alone on an empty platform."

Julian got up and put the syphon into his bag. "So we've reached an understanding?"

"We have. Both of us."

In the vestibule downstairs, Leizor sat on the floor, playing. He was laying out coins in two rows, the small coins in one, the larger coins in the other.

"What are you doing?" asked Julian.

"Counting money."

"But you don't know how to count."

"I do."

"Get up, nudnik, we're going shopping."

And right at that moment Julian felt a faintness, a fear. He sat in a chair and leaned back. His fear grew, making him sweat. He unbuttoned his coat, took off his hat, and put it on the side table.

"Ready," said Leizor, getting up from the floor.

Julian was angry. "Wait, damn you! In such a hurry. We're not going. I don't feel well. . . . And do you know why? Of course you don't. You don't understand anything, and you're happy. Whereas I understand everything, and I'm miserable." He hit the table with his fist. "Mr. Bodol suffers! He doesn't know what he is—but I know! He's a good man, but he thinks he has defiled himself beyond repair. He'll think that to the end of his life. And I suffer because I see this and can't help him."

"You will drink vodka," said Leizor very distinctly.

"He doesn't understand a thing, the nudnik, but he knows I'll drink. . . . I can't today, with the shopping to do."

The dog Misiek, who had been lying in the corner by the window, got up lazily and went over to Julian. Wagging his tail, he sniffed Julian's shoes.

"And you know, too?" Julian marveled.

"I am not going to bring you any more bottles," said Leizor. "No more. You buy them yourself. . . ."

"Enough, Leizor, I have to rest. We'll talk later."

Julian got up, paced, sat down again. He knew that in a few minutes, when he felt better, he would go to the nearest bar and have a shot of vodka, then another, then a third. And then he'd buy a bottle of the vodka with the red label and sit down on a lonely bench blackened by rain and snow, but comfortable, wide enough. He could see that bench now, and the Vistula flowing below.

The water is gray, the sky is gray, and so are the houses of Praga. A steamer moves slowly on the river, her deck full of people. One can hear music from loudspeakers mounted somewhere on board, and Julian feels sure that people are dancing on the boat. Yes, there are sure to be young couples dancing, maybe older couples too, people his age. He imagines himself dancing with Rivka. As they dance, they rise into the air above the boat, above the river and city, hovering, as in that picture by Marc Chagall. Julian has a print of it in his room at home. The print hangs over his bed, reminding him of the day he married Rachel, who starved to death in the Lwów ghetto. But now Julian floats through the air with Rivka, and they float toward a small town where long ago Rivka baked cream rolls and her husband Abram topped them with poppy seeds and sold them for five groszy apiece in a little shop that was clean as a whistle and as white as the best-grade wheat flour. The picture fades suddenly, though, and Julian is sad to see it vanish just at the point when he and Rivka arrived at that little town. He squints, but the picture doesn't return; instead he hears voices. It is Leizor talking to the dog, and the dog is answering with yips and barks.

The nurse Lodzia crossed the hall.

Julian called her. "Come here, dear. Won't you come over to a poor Jew?"

"Yes, Julian, what can I do?"

"Miss Lodzia, and you, Miss Leokadia, it's a good thing you're here. You're in the nick of time. Take my money, my briefcase, my hat, please. You understand. . . . I need to sleep. . . . Someone else will have to buy the seltzer, the chicken, the challah. . . ."

Julian took some crumpled bills out of his trouser pocket and pressed them into the first nurse's hand. Then he turned out the pockets of his coat, took out a handful of coins, some crushed cigarettes, and a matchbox, and put it all on the side table. A few coins fell to the floor. Leizor picked them up and handed them to Miss Lodzia. "He wants to buy a bottle," he said, "but he can't now, without the money."

"That's all right, don't worry, Leizor," Miss Lodzia said soothingly. "We'll take Julian to his room."

"I can go myself," said Julian. Slowly, as if by some careful plan, he made for the elevator.

Miss Lodzia stepped aside to let Julian and Leizor pass, then closed the elevator door. Leizor pressed the button marked "2nd floor," and the cage rose out of sight.

The Viper

Felicja slammed the door, locked it, and sat on the bed. They wouldn't write her prescriptions, the high-and-mighty physicians and professors. She wasn't to take this medicine, that drug, she was not permitted to swallow such-and-such a pill! What did they know? Nothing! She shook her fist at the door. She would show them! She choked on her saliva, coughed, said: "Bastards! I'm sick! A lot sicker than Itzik or Menachem, Jadzia or Maria, Rachel or Avrum. To hell with you!"

In the room a lamp was on, and through the wide-open window moths flew in and circled it, now disappearing in the shadows, now reappearing near the bulb.

"Out of my room, bugs!" She seized a folded newspaper and went to work on the insects, cursing. She was in a temper and at first didn't hear the knocking at the door. "Who's that?"

"It's me."

"Who's me?"

"Bela."

"Which Bela?"

"There's only one." The woman's voice became more distinct. "Bela Rein."

Felicja opened the door, let Bela in, and turned the key in the lock again.

"They have a second key," said Bela, sitting on a chair.

"Let them . . ."

"Don't be angry, Felicja." Bela took a pack of cigarettes from her bag, lit one, and inhaled deeply. "I dream of a decent cigarette, like a Nile or an Egyptian . . . those were smokes!"

"Did you smoke before the War?"

"Oh, yes."

"Then you must have been a prostitute."

"Felicja, what are you saying?"

"Ladies didn't smoke, didn't wear makeup, didn't wave their hair, and didn't do a lot of things that are done every day now in the street, in the line at the banana stand."

"What things?"

"Women pluck their eyebrows and draw black lines in their place. They paint their eyelids green and wear outlandish rings on their fingers. In our apartment house there was a Dvoira Greitzer. They called her Dvoira the Redhead because of her copper hair, and she wore so many rings, they also called her the Ring Lady. Her lips were scarlet with lipstick, her cheeks were rouged, and for her eyebrows I think she used black shoe polish."

"Well, I'm not Dvoira Greitzer," Bela said, "and I don't put shoe polish on my eyebrows. I'm here, anyway, on official business."

"What official business?" asked Felicja. With the newspaper she swatted at a white moth that was making for the lamp. "I'll kill you, filthy thing! They pester the life out of me."

"I've come," Bela Rein continued, "regarding the matter of your brother Henryk."

"I have no brother," Felicja shouted, wielding the newspaper again at an approaching moth.

"Henryk is ill, he needs help," Bela said. "He *must* be helped."

"I don't know any Henryk."

"You know one—and know him well."

"For me he is dead!" Felicja paced. "What sort of official business is this, anyway?"

"I'm a social worker." Bela took a folder of papers and a pen from her bag. "I'm here to conduct a social-welfare interview with you on the topic of Mr. Henryk Gorczewski."

"Since when are you a social worker?"

"For years."

"You never mentioned it before."

"I'm mentioning it now."

"Come on, Bela, we've known each other—"

"I'm here officially." Bela Rein unfolded a blank form on the table. "Your name, please, first and last, and date of birth."

Felicja lay down on the bed. "I'm feeling worse, I'm going to die soon."

"I need this information!"

"But you know me, you're my friend. . . ."

"Please answer the question." Bela raised her voice.

"All right, all right! Felicja Anna Gorczewski, maiden name Kowarski. My mama's name was Maria, my dad's name was Jan. I'm in my sixties."

"How old exactly? Please be precise."

"Seventy-three, then, damn you!"

"Good. Seventy-three . . ."

"You want my whole life story?"

"Yes, we need a broad overview of this case."

"A what?"

"A broad overview."

"Bela, you're beginning to make me sorry I know you, sorry I let you in my room. Is it a viper I've been protecting in my bosom?"

"Who's a viper? Who?" Bela hit the table with her fist. "Is this the respect you show an official social worker? You insult me personally, too, but that I forgive you."

"You mean—you're writing all this down?"

"Of course I am!"

"Well, in that case I beg your pardon." Felicja drew a tin box out from under a cushion, sat down, and opened it. "Help yourself, Bela dear, these are very good mints. . . ." She set the box on the table.

"You can't bribe me with candy. Now, I want your life story, and your brother's."

"I'll speak for myself, he can speak for himself."

"Then speak."

"I *am* speaking! I was born in the village of Wielka Wola. My father had a few acres of land, one cow, and some hogs and rabbits. At my baptism my godmother was Janina Nowak and my godfather, Roman Janiak. When my parents died, my little brother and I were raised by the priest's housekeeper. . . . The parsonage burned down during an air raid."

"Felicja!"

"What, Bela?"

"You're making this up."

"That's my official life story," Felicja said heatedly. "I have two life stories, one for myself, the other for you people. Leave mine alone, or I'll . . . No, wait." Felicja began to cough.

"Have a mint," Bela said, offering her the tin box. "It'll help."

"To hell with your mints," Felicja said, coughing.

"But they're your mints."

"I don't care whose they are."

"Calm down, Felicja. I understand. You're upset."

"You don't understand. I'm double, there are two Felicjas, the outside one, the inside one. It drives me crazy. Do I have to talk about it?"

"Yes."

"I haven't told anyone, since the War. . . . My parents' real names were Rachel and Leizor Nachman. I was born in Warsaw. I remember everything! The house, the streets, the courtyard, the stairs, the rail for carpet-beating, the wooden trash barrel, and the outhouse in back with the little sign on the door saying 'See Porter for Key.' And the porter, Wacław, had consumption, and Genowefa, his wife, was pockmarked and made love in the cellar with Wacław's younger brother, whose name was Bonifacy. I remember the organ grinder Michałek and his parrot, and a gang of children: Chaimek, the two Aarons, Halinka, Pesia, Shimon, Romek, and Moniek, who was freckled. I remember how Father pulled my ear to punish me, how Granny Rivka made preserves for me, how Mama kissed me good night in my small bed. But what use, Bela, are those memories to me now?

"Put down in your official form that I had golden curls

which later darkened, that Mama used to tie a red bow in my hair, that in elementary school I stuck my tongue out at the teacher and Father spanked me, and then I was a young lady, and then . . . And then I had to go into hiding, being the mortal enemy of National Socialism and the German Army and the police.

"Write all that down, please, and then go away, because I'm sick and there's nobody to bring me a glass of water or take my temperature, with all the doctors and young ladies in white here. Write that I'm dying because they refuse to help me, because they don't know how to help."

"I'll write what has to be written, but about Henryk I still have not heard a thing."

"Stop nagging me, Bela! You're as bad a pest as these moths. Now that you're an official person, you have no sympathy for someone who is seriously ill."

"I was delegated here in the matter of your brother."

"Delegated. Another of those words. What, am I supposed to kneel down and worship? Well, I don't receive delegations. I invite people in, or I tell them to go to hell!"

"Calm yourself, Felicja, I have to get this done, don't you see?"

"All right. What do you want?"

"I want to help your brother."

"Then help him!" Felicja was angry.

"But you're his sister, you ought to help take care of him."

"I'm sick, you don't seem to understand that!"

"You're in better health than he is."

"He has no sister," Felicja said. She took the box of candy from the table, held it for a moment, and put it back under the cushion. "You don't like mints?" she asked.

"I don't like lies," said Bela Rein, and lit another cigarette.

"Cross your legs now, that's all you need to look like Dvoira Greitzer," Felicja sneered.

"Why, Felicja, don't you want to help your brother? You're in an institution, too, but you could move in with your brother anytime. He has a nice apartment there and wants you to be with him. You are still strong, the two of you could live together. I spoke with your physicians, and they agree with my assessment."

"Your what?"

"My assessment of the case."

"Another word I don't know."

"So what do you say?" Bela was growing impatient.

"Are you deaf? Have I been mumbling? He has no sister! *You* go to him, *you* live with him."

Bela put the forms back into her bag. "Frankly, I have considered that. I always liked him."

"You always liked him, did you? Ah? Now you just wait a minute, you snake in the grass, you bureaucrat in skirts, you big-deal social worker, you just wait a minute, little righteous Bela, I have something to tell you. Listen to what Felicja of the Nachman family, a good family, has to tell you now." Felicja took the box out from under the cushion, opened it, picked a mint, and put it into her mouth. She sucked it for a while, then said: "Henryk Gorczewski isn't my brother, he's my husband. We were married by the town rabbi in nineteen thirty."

"What? What?" Bela jumped up, then sat down again, but the chair wasn't there, it had turned over, so she fell to the floor. "God!" she moaned. "Now I've broken my back, and it's your fault, you and that Henryk of yours!"

"Look at her, will you, she fell from the fifth floor and snapped her spine. Get up, or I'll call the orderlies."

"I can't get up."

"Well, then sit there and listen to the rest of it. In nineteen thirty I married Chaim Brun—that's the real name of the Henryk who caught your fancy all of a sudden. And if it hadn't been for the War, the Occupation, and the Ghetto, he and I would have been a normal married couple. But now, because of this crazy world, we are anything but normal. We wangled papers for ourselves . . . ah, if only we could have got the *right* kind of papers. . . . Good people on the other side of the Ghetto wall did their best, but they could only arrange it in the way they did. You understand?"

"No."

"Chaim and I became brother and sister: Miss Felicja Anna Gorczewska and Mr. Henryk Józef Gorczewski, residing on the Aryan side of the wall with the Listewkis, relatives of theirs from a remote village which had been completely destroyed by fire in nineteen thirty-nine. . . . But that wasn't the end of it. My Chaim-Henryk, it so happens, makes a hit with the young lady next door, and she begins to make eyes at him. And makes eyes and makes eyes, until my dear Chaim-Henryk softens and gives in. He goes off with his lady now here, now there, and I see it but can't say a word, because of the Occupation, you understand. . . ."

"Yes, Felicja, I understand everything, but I can't get up."

"Then sit and listen!" She bent over Bela Rein. "Right in front of me she would kiss him, or say to me: 'What a wonderful brother you have! Handsome as Gary Cooper and elegant as Adam Brodzisz.' That's how she talked, and my insides turned over and over. She was a good woman, she helped us, but we didn't dare tell her the truth. She brought us pork from her aunt in the country, butter, a hen, eggs, honey, and occasionally greens. One Sunday Henryk announced that he had joined. That was the word they used then, 'joined.' So he told me that if he didn't come home someday, it would mean that he had left Warsaw for the forest. And the next day, he didn't come home. Later I learned that Henryk's lady friend hadn't come home either. Just the two of us were left, Mrs. Listewki and I, because Mr. Listewki was caught in an SS street roundup. They sent him to Germany, to do forced labor. Those were hard times."

"They certainly were." Bela made an effort to get up. She held out her hand to Felicja and with her other arm pushed herself up slowly from the floor. "Please," she said, grunting, "help me, Felicja."

Felicja took Bela's hand, but then got her leg caught on the dresser and, pulled by Bela, fell, and both women sat down hard on the floor, side by side. From the open dresser drawer tumbled white, green, and pink pills, small envelopes and bottles of medicine. Something herbal spilled or broke, and a dark fluid seeped through a cardboard container. The lamp was knocked onto the bed, where it continued shedding light, though much less. The moths all fled.

"You . . . you Dvoira Greitzer, you! Look what you've done!" Felicja raged. "Destroyed, in one second, what it took me months to save! Get out!"

"Ah," said Bela, "this will be reported. That you hoard medicine and are strong as a bull!"

"You won't tell."

"I will."

"You won't."

"I must. It's my duty."

"Bela, I know you want to hear about Henryk, so listen," Felicja said in a low voice as she began to collect the scattered pills and envelopes and put them back into the drawer. "When the War ended, I went to live in Prushków. Every morning I took the train to Warsaw, where I worked, and returned in the evening. One day, I returned and found Henryk waiting for me in my room. He greeted me very tenderly, kissed me, we had supper together, and then he said, 'I'm sorry, Felicja, but I have another wife. We were in the Resistance together and there is nothing I can do about it now. Ewa is going to have a baby. I still love you, but I love Ewa, too, and the baby that is coming.' "

Felicja stopped. She got down on her stomach and reached under the bed for some scattered pills and bottles.

"And what happened then?" asked Bela.

"Nothing."

"You mean he stayed with her, and you remained alone?"

"Yes." Felicja got up from the floor, brushed herself off, put the dresser back in its place, and inserted the drawer. "There is a little more." She took Bela's arm, helped her up onto the bed, and herself sat down in the chair. "Ewa died a week after the birth of the baby, and their son is now abroad. The construction company he works for sends him abroad for a year or sometimes more. He is a nice boy, but as for Henryk, I have broken off with him forever, he is neither husband nor brother to me. . . . And I advise you not to get involved with him. He has no heart. He uses women like gloves."

"Felicja, you don't know what you're saying . . ."

"Or, rather, he changes women like gloves."

Bela rose, went to the window, took a deep breath, then turned back, clutched her bag, and announced:

"Tomorrow, at 5 P.M., we'll go to see him together and settle this matter once and for all: either you stay there or I move in with him. Take your choice!"

"I'm not going."

Bela went to the door, unlocked it, and with her hand on the knob, said gaily, "In that case, good-bye, Felicja."

"You can go to hell, my dear Bela, you can go straight to hell."

Bela Rein nodded and quickly shut the door behind her.

Trouble Sleeping

Mateusz is in Room 213. Ewa is in Room 214. A wall divides them.

The attendant tells Ewa: "The boy in two-thirteen had visitors today, two ladies and two gentlemen, and later, a man with a goatee."

The nurse tells Mateusz: "Your neighbor in two-fourteen ate her lunch today. We have a lot of trouble with her. She eats like a mouse, smokes cigarettes, and reads all the time."

Mateusz smiles and says: "Mice eat a lot. Do you have any idea how much grain a mouse can eat?"

Ewa often hears Mateusz cough. At night, when everybody is asleep, she lifts her head and listens. Ewa pictures Mateusz: lanky, a dark complexion, a hooked nose, brown eyes, a shock of black hair. Hands composed on the white counterpane.

Mateusz was a pianist. He performed on famous stages, and the audiences shouted bravo. Perhaps Ewa had seen him, when she went on a class trip to a Chopin concert. She slept through half the concert, because she was tired and had a fever, from tonsillitis. But in the thirtieth row she had not seen the pianist clearly. So it might have been Mateusz.

"I can lift my arms, move my hands, but he can't any-more," Ewa thinks, clenching her fists, and hits the blanket. In the night, a bell sounds. Someone somewhere is asking for a bedpan. There is movement in the hall. A sleepy attendant comes running, or it might be a nurse on her way to call the doctor. The ringing might come from the ward where the terminal cases are.

The nights are eventful, and every night is different. Last night, for example, there was a ring at one o'clock, and for quite a while the attendant was busy carrying urinals back and forth in the men's ward. When one has to go, they all have to go. About three o'clock, a nurse, giving somebody an IV, called out: "Ela, bring me a decent tube!" At four, Ewa was roused by a conversation in the hall between an attendant and a nurse. Then, toward morning, Anitowicz in 222 started shouting at someone. Anitowicz does not sleep at night, he wanders through the wards, knocks over bedside stands, turns on faucets, and then gets into someone else's bed, which causes a great commotion and cries for help.

There used to be a certain Mrs. Bogacki, who did without beds altogether. She would make herself a pallet on the floor. Once she approached Ewa and said, "Honey, take me in, let's live together." Ewa put her finger on the bell and kept it there until an attendant rushed in, alarmed, because Ewa rang very rarely, only if she became dizzy or fell out of bed, which happened twice. The head nurse suggested attaching safety rungs to the bed at night, but Ewa refused: she wasn't going to live in a cage.

Mateusz would fall asleep only toward morning and then

sleep through breakfast, which always upset Roma, the cook. "Warmed-over breakfast again for lunch . . . What do the dietician and the doctor have to say about that, I'd like to know?" Roma tempted Mateusz with various goodies—cheesecake, shortbread, sometimes a piece of torte—which she swore were homemade, but everyone knew that she bought them in a pastry shop.

She spoiled Mateusz. "You're my favorite, because you're from Lwów and I'm from Lwów," she often told him with affection. "You know something, Mateusz?" she said to him one day. "On the other side of this wall lies a girl. She's twenty. The day before yesterday, she asked about you. A pretty girl, she has lovely long hair. She won't let them trim it, she says it's her only fortune. The attendants comb her hair every morning. Mateusz, you never saw such hair! And it's hard to put in braids, the hair just slips away from you, it's so fine and delicate. In the sun it shines like gold!"

That night, falling asleep earlier than usual, Ewa had a bad dream. She heard shouts, moans, people weeping. Someone seized her by the hair and pulled, giving her a terrible headache. She woke up and found herself in darkness and on the floor. When her head cleared, she reached out and took hold of the bed frame and with difficulty pulled herself up. She cursed her useless legs. Scrambling into the bed, clutching the sheets, she knocked the pillow to the floor. Then the blanket slid off and hit the night table, which fell over with a loud bang.

In the square of light from the open door stood the nurse Marta.

"Nothing's wrong," said Ewa. "The night table fell over,

because the blanket they've given me is filthy, frayed, and everything around here is poor quality. . . ."

Marta righted the table and asked the attendant to remake Ewa's bed. Ewa could not stand Marta, and by now everyone knew it. The nurse was pretty, had a good figure, and often looked in on Mateusz. Too often, Ewa felt.

One day, when Ewa was being wheeled past the nurses' desk, she heard Marta saying, "Mateusz has a noble profile, and nice eyes." Ewa herself had never seen Mateusz's face. When she went past his room and the door was open, she sometimes leaned out of her chair, but could see only the white of the sheets, sometimes Mateusz's motionless hand, or two feet sticking out at the foot of the bed. "Even his feet have a nice shape," she thought. "Except they're a little yellowish." And now Marta was standing over her. People always stood over Ewa, whether she was in her bed or her wheelchair.

"Are you feeling all right, Ewa?"

"Me? I'm fine. I don't need anything. . . ."

"You're upset."

Ewa hated Marta's always-clean uniform, the little white cap with black piping that went so well with her dark complexion.

"I don't want to look at you," Ewa choked out. "You're too pretty."

"Ewa, I can't help my looks. But you, too . . . You know how we all admire your lovely hair, your patience, your knowledge."

"Disgusting, oh, she is disgusting!" Ewa thought. "I don't want her pity, her half-witted pity."

Mateusz woke up when the attendant Frania came in with a bowl of warm water. She washed his face, ears, and neck. Then she fed him.

"Frania, I love you," said Mateusz.

"Sure, sure."

"I do!"

"Careful, you'll choke on your food."

"Frania!"

"What?"

"Let me kiss you."

"Kiss the dog's nose." But she leaned forward. "Here, on the cheek, you rascal!" She stroked his forehead, then. "You're smart, but where has it got you?"

"I've traveled around the world, seen many people . . . in New York, for example."

"You played the piano there?"

"Once I was sitting at the fountain by the Metropolitan Opera and I saw two old ladies, twins, dressed in identical ermine jackets. When they went down the steps, they opened their handbags, also identical, and approached a man playing a violin."

"What was he playing?"

"A capriccio by Paganini . . . And on the sidewalk in front of him was his hat, into which people dropped coins. The two old ladies bent over and put a dollar each into the hat. The violinist stopped, raised his bow, and waited. The ladies, conferring with each other, dropped another dollar each. But still the violinist didn't play. The ladies put their heads together again and reached a decision. One of them carefully removed the four dollar bills from the hat and replaced them with a ten-dollar bill. The violinist smiled, nodded, and continued playing. He played beautifully, and when he finished, he bowed. The old ladies waved good-bye to him and got into a white Mercedes. "I went up to the violinist then and told him that I liked his playing. 'I was at your concert yesterday,' he replied. 'I love Chopin. My grandmother was from Poland.' "

"What's the Metropolitan Opera?"

"They put on operas and ballets there. Like the Grand Theatre in Warsaw."

"Ah. Well, I have to go now. Be good, dear."

In the hall Frania ran into Marta.

"Well, and how is our Mateusz?" Marta asked.

"An angel of a boy, an angel!"

Ewa has just had breakfast and is waiting for the attendant. It is Frania today, thinks Ewa. A hard worker, Frania, and nice to talk to.

"Well, and how has our little one slept?" asks Frania, entering.

"Not well. I dreamt that someone hit me over the head and pulled my hair."

Frania starts combing Ewa's hair. "Sit up, love! There, that's better, and don't twist. I just came from Mateusz."

"And how did he sleep?" Ewa asks.

"He slept well. Don't turn."

"And who is with him now?"

"Marta."

"But Marta had the night shift!"

"It isn't over yet."

"She always hangs around there."

"Everyone looks in on him, the doctor, the nurses, the

attendants. . . . They look in on you, too. Don't wriggle, you'll get an elf-lock."

"Frania?"

"What?"

"You won't tell anybody?"

"I won't."

"I dreamt I had a baby."

"That's nice, but children mean trouble. . . ."

"And did *he* dream anything?"

"Oh, yes. He dreamt he was in New York and played at the Metropolitan Opera, in an auditorium filled with thousands of people. And after the concert two handsome young ladies, twins, wearing ermine, invited him to dinner. And at the restaurant a violinist played at their table, and the violinist's grandmother was Polish."

"That was his dream? You're lying!"

"Cross my heart!"

"And then what happened?"

"Then he woke up."

"Poor Mateusz," Ewa whispers.

"There we are, now. End of beauty treatment."

Frania gets up. Ewa snuggles down into the bed. "Thank you, Frania," she murmurs, smiling.

Snapshot

Dora Sharf had a large black handbag secured by two locks. In the evening, just before going to sleep, she would open the bag and spread out all its contents on the rug by her bed. Groaning and wheezing, she would sit on the hassock and take each object one by one, inspect it, and put it back into the bag. First, her combs. A black comb, the prewar one with three missing teeth, she slipped into the inner side pocket. A green comb, somewhat smaller, went into the same place, but not as deeply, so she could pull it out by feel and without effort. Then there was a little white comb she never used, calling it her spare. Its place was the very bottom of the bag.

In the little round mirror Dora looked at her nose, then at one eye, then at the other; she pushed out her lips and made faces. Tonight, she decided, she would change handkerchiefs. She put aside the green-and-gray handkerchief and from under a pillow took out a stack of clean, white, glossy ones, all folded and monogrammed, and stowed them in the bag next to the pocket with the combs. These were the handkerchiefs of her husband, Solomon Sharf, who was killed in 1942 near the Ghetto wall. A large framed photograph of Solomon hung over Dora's bed: an enlargement from a damaged snapshot, made in 1959 by Michael Fiszel, whom Dora had known before the War.

In the picture Solomon Sharf was a balding, dark-haired man with bushy eyebrows, a cheerful smile, and ears that stuck out. When Michael brought it to her, he said: "I didn't realize Sol's ears stuck out so much." At first Dora took offense, but later, when she made her peace with the fact that she had had a husband with big ears, she said: "He was what he was, and I can't say anything bad about him. He was a decent Jew, and died like others in those years."

Next Dora took a silver teaspoon, a fork, a soup spoon, and a small knife, and put them into a little linen pouch, which also went into the handbag.

"Yes, yes," she said, turning to the portrait of her husband, "you look at me and say nothing, although you know that I got this sterling set from your dear sister Shaindla, and now look what's left of it." She pulled the linen pouch back out, considered it for a moment, then again pushed it to the bottom of the handbag. "Listen, Solomon, I'm not complaining. Really! You always kept up your hope that Hitler would lose. And he did lose. But so did you, and so did I. You lost your life, and I lost you. And our house. What, you ask, was I able to preserve? I'll tell you: it's all in this handbag. Here is my fortune . . . two gold coins, two earrings, a silver cigarette case engraved 'To Solomon from Dora,' a silver signet, and three wedding rings. Why three? Because I bought an extra one, just in case. . . . Don't get angry, I'm saving for a gravestone for you. Where am I going to put the gravestone? Don't worry, I know where. Do you remember the little town where you were born? Remember, Solomon? We were there, visiting your parents. Your mama wasn't happy about your choosing a Warsaw girl. Don't interrupt. I know better than you. Your wife was to be Ruchla, and you don't even know that Ruchla has survived and lives in this neighborhood, and we often talk about this. Oh yes, she is still jealous of me, because she had to marry Shlamek Bylic, the tailor who swore."

Dora sighed and again began to root among the objects scattered on the rug. She chose a silver-plated compact, opened it, took out the powder puff, and waved it a few times in the air. A pink dust rose, then settled on the floor. With a finger Dora wrote "Solomon" in it.

Ah, Solomon, why did you have to go to that wall? You were always pigheaded. Shlamek Bylic, too, left Ruchla a widow. He was killed at the front. But Michael Fiszel escaped from a transport headed for Treblinka and still lives. Solomon, listen to me. I can't be alone anymore. Michael comes from a good family. He is like you in a way: stubborn. And he's intelligent, clean, shaves every day, and is punctual. But can you imagine, Ruchla is up to her old tricks, trying to snatch him away from me. But I know you won't say anything. You never did. You were never one for giving advice. You always said: "Dora, dear, do as you think right," and Dora dear did as she thought right, and if it turned out to be wrong, you shrugged and said it wasn't your fault. You men . . . !

But when Michael sits next to me, I feel good. I talk, he listens. He talks, I listen. And he talks beautifully, and that is very important. Once he told me how his grandmother Esther lost her wits.

"Older people turn foolish," he said, "because it often seems to them that they are younger than they are. Their brains order one thing to be done, but their arms and legs do something quite different. In the brain arises the thought: 'I am going to dance a little waltz now.' The legs, however, unprepared for such a thought, can't move the rest of the body right, so the person hops awkwardly, comically, and ends up sprawling on the floor.

"Grandma Esther met a young fellow who sold used books. It was a modest business; the young man was no Mortkowicz, Rój, or Gebethner and Wolf. Anyway, my grandmother, while she was marketing, often stopped at Mr. Silber's book stand. There was also a Mr. Silber Senior, the father of Silber Junior. The father would take over for the son when the son was either out buying books or preparing lunch at home, which was on Franciszkańska Street, or moonlighting as a part-time gravedigger at the cemetery on Gęsia Street. One fine day, I noticed my grandmother on Franciszkańska Street, and behind her walked Mr. Silber Junior. They stopped at the gate, looked around, then ducked in quickly. . . ."

Dora burst out laughing. Ah, Solomon! Why am I telling you this? You know life, you understand Michael Fiszel's grandmother. . . . I need to be understood, too. Do you approve, Solomon? You do, don't you? What a dear you are. . . . Well, now I have some tidying up to do, and some shopping.

She put the rest of the things back into her bag, got up, and stretched. There was a sudden pain in her left side. But the pain passed. She went to the bathroom and turned on the faucets. The water rushed into the tub while Dora, smiling at her reflection in the mirror, took the pins out of her full hair, which was dyed blonde.

Michael Fiszel, meanwhile, was sitting on a sofa next to Ruchla Bylic.

"It's not my fault that Solomon was my friend," said Michael. "And he was a good friend. As if there could be bad friends . . . In any case, he remains in our memory."

"In *your* memory." Ruchla smiled at him.

"Not only in mine, dear Ruchla. He also remains in his widow's memory. She continues to love and honor him. . . ."

"And so you want to marry this widow."

"One has a certain duty, an obligation," he faltered. "It is . . . I find it difficult to express. . . . She needs care, protection, good advice."

"You like her, that's all." Ruchla took a handkerchief out of the cuff of her left sleeve and wiped invisible tears from her cheeks. "And I have been waiting for you all these years. Waiting for you to make up your mind."

"Let's be sensible, dear Ruchla. . . ."

"I'm not that old, that I have to be sensible. I'm a woman and you're a man, and if anything is left in us from those days . . ."

"We should preserve it," Michael concluded lamely.

"As long as possible, dear Michael!" Ruchla said, nodding, and turned to him. "Kiss me on the cheek, apologize, and then let's drop the subject."

He kissed her on the cheek, took a white envelope from a side pocket of his suit, and put it down on the table nearby.

"What's this?" Ruchla asked.

"Photographs of us," Michael said.

"When did you take them? I don't remember. . . ."

"In nineteen thirty-eight." From the envelope he took three large pictures and a smaller one. "I made copies from this old snapshot. See? I pressed it, put a back on it, retouched it, did enlargements. The prints are as good as new. There's you, Dora, Solomon, Sarah, and myself."

"Sarah? I don't remember a Sarah. . . ."

"Sarah Rozmaryn!"

"Oh! The tall one who wanted to steal Shlamek from me? Yes, I remember her. I walked into my Shlamek's room, and there she was sitting next to him, as close as I am sitting to you now, and she was saying: 'You sew and polish so beautifully, one could fall in love with your beautiful tailor's hands.' "

"What she meant—"

"I don't want to hear it! I couldn't stand her. And one day at the market, she upped the price of a hen on me. . . . The farm woman was asking two zlotys, I offered one-thirty, the woman came down to one-eighty, I went up twenty groszy to one-fifty, and she was just on the point of agreeing to one-sixty when Sarah Rozmaryn barged in, saying, 'Here's one-seventy. I'll take that hen.' So I paid two zlotys quick and put the hen under my arm, so she couldn't have it."

"But she was—"

"Don't tell me she was beautiful. The whole shtetl went on and on about how beautiful she was. I was sick of hearing it. I don't know what people saw in her."

"I was going to say, Ruchla dear, that she was hanged by the Nazis. She was the first victim in our town. They beat her with rifle butts, then hanged her on the main street, on a tree next to the rabbi's house. It was because they found, in her room, a Polish soldier's uniform and some papers. The story was that this soldier was the son of our pharmacist, Wojtek Suwalski."

"Now, Wojtek Suwalski was a good person," Ruchla said. "He helped the poor, he gave medicine on credit."

"Sarah—"

"Well, the Rozmaryn girl wasn't so bad, either."

"Not bad, yes."

"And, actually, she *was* beautiful. And Wojtek, I remember, was a handsome man. He used to ride a black mare. The mare, Karusia, had a white patch, a star on her forehead. Her coat always glistened, and she held her head high. On a meadow beyond the river, near the Gołębiarz farm, Wojtek set up hurdles out of planks and branches, and Karusia jumped over them. With each jump, Wojtek shouted. The whole town knew when he was riding his mare, they could hear his shouts over the river, you could hear him as far as Garncarska Lane, where Sarah Rozmaryn lived. Sometimes I saw her standing at the window. Perhaps she was watching Wojtek on his Karusia."

"That's possible," said Michael with a sigh. "It's too bad I don't have a photograph of Wojtek, or of the other people of our little town. Once, before the War, I suggested that every year our photographer, Mr. Zając on Kościelna Street, should take a group picture of all of us and display it in his store window. He laughed at me. So I bought a secondhand camera and told my mother that I was going to open a photographic studio. She laughed at me. Now I have two expensive cameras, the latest equipment, light meters, an enlarger, but the people are gone."

"There are other people," observed Ruchla.

"And I take their pictures, of course." Michael got up. "Time for me to go. Don't forget, Dora Sharf invited us to dinner tomorrow."

"I won't forget, but Dora might." Ruchla got up, too, and stood close to Michael. "Don't do anything rash, Michael. Give it thought."

"I have given it thought," he said softly, and kissed Ruchla on the forehead. "Good-bye, dear."

She sat down again and said firmly, "You'll come back to me. I'll be waiting."

On the stairs, Michael Fiszel remembered that he had left the snapshot and three prints on the table. He did not turn back, but continued walking down unhurriedly.

Forty-nine Visits

Nurse Maria made an effort to pierce the vein in the patient's right wrist with her needle. "It's garbage, not a needle," she muttered. "Dull, the bastard's dull."

The sick woman smiled. "I'm dying, it doesn't matter," she whispered. "Let it be dull."

"What are you talking about, Helena? You'll live to be a hundred." The nurse hit the vein and slowly pushed in the plunger of the syringe. "This will help you get back on your feet. . . . We are giving you a whole series of these. But the bedpan has to be scrubbed, the smell from it is no joke. I'll tell the aide to do it right away. Let's open the window wider, it's warm outside, sunshine, good fresh air. . . . You mustn't worry, dear, your room will be like a little treasure box, I'll see to that. They'll change the sheets tomorrow. I'll send Krystyna to help you eat. You like Krystyna, she's a good aide. . . ."

The sick woman narrowed her eyes. Maria pulled the needle out quickly and pressed a wad of cotton in its place.

"Well, what do you say? Feeling better?"

"I don't know. I didn't know dying would be so difficult. . . . Please don't look at me. I don't want anyone to look at me."

I sat down in a chair by the bed. The nurse straightened the patient's bedding and left.

"You should drink more, you know, you should drink a lot," I told Helena.

"My body is hideous, my face repulsive, and I used to be pretty, yes. Or so people said. . . . I stayed unmarried to keep my beauty, to be myself. . . . And I was myself. . . ."

"Hold on to that thought to the end," I said.

She smiled. "These wrinkles, this sagging flesh. The fingernails still grow, and the bedding has to be changed, and the smell . . ."

"You were yourself, you were happy."

"True, those were good years. There was a man . . . No one knows about that. It happened suddenly. He was older than I, a lot older, but for us it was always spring. I met him in winter, though . . . But I've said enough . . . I talk too much."

I got up and made for the door.

"Seven years of happiness . . . seven biblical years. It was before the War. You're leaving?"

I stopped. "You are tired."

"Yes, this is hard, but it can't be helped. I realize now that the silence tormented me. I told no one about him . . . Please, sit here next to me."

I turned back, put the chair closer to the bed, and sat down.

"I was twenty-five at the time and I wanted love, but when my wish was fulfilled, I found that I still wanted love. . . . It is a thirst that cannot be quenched. . . . We were together only seven years. He left."

"Was there someone else? Did you find someone else?"

Helena smiled, and I had the impression that she welcomed my question.

"I will tell you . . . if you have the time . . ."

"Certainly," I assured her.

"It was a very long time ago . . . You see, it begins like a fairy tale. . . . So, once upon a time, beyond the forests and mountains, in a lovely city in Europe occupied by the German army, a city rich in antiquities, palaces, churches, museums, high buildings, and a magnificent cathedral, there lived, on one of the streets, in a tiny windowless room in an attic, Princess Helena."

"You . . . ?"

"None other . . . At night I went out on the roof to breathe some fresh air. I went to bed at dawn and woke up around noon. I kept track of the days and months by drawing slashes and stars on a wall. A slash was a day, a star a month. Sundays and holidays I marked by horizontal lines; days that were special for any reason were marked by a little circle. On the hundred forty-third day, the door of my cell was opened by a young man, who said: 'I am with the police, but don't be afraid, I will help you. I'll tell the people who sent me here that I checked the attic but found nothing. Your hiding place is well-camouflaged, you need not fear.' With that, he left and carefully closed the door after him. From that time on, I tensely waited, dreading the day when he would return and instead of 'You need not fear' say 'Out with you.' Or tell me to face the wall, take his pistol out, and shoot me right there, in the back of the head. Several days passed. . . .

"'He came one evening and stood in the doorway with my landlady beside him. I lit a candle and saw his face, his smile, the bright eyes and noble forehead. I told myself that surely I could trust him. 'If you need to send a letter somewhere, I can arrange it. Please don't be afraid,' he said. My landlady nodded her head to that, and her, of course, I trusted completely. He came more often. He would give five light knocks at my door, then two harder ones. . . . That was our signal. We would sit side by side. He spoke little, I was silent. His visits were short, only a few minutes. He brought things: an apple, a piece of jelly roll, an orange, an onion, or a few cloves of garlic. Whatever it was, he put it down on the straw mattress on which we sat and said '*Bon appétit.*'

"'One day he asked me what I planned to do after the War. I answered: 'I'll lie in the sun.' 'And what else?' he asked. 'I'll eat some crisp buttered kaiser rolls and write an essay about the Good Man.' That is how I answered him then, for that is how I felt. As time went on, I stopped being afraid, I became calmer. I was still vigilant, my hearing was sharp, and I reacted to every rustle, the least sound, but my perpetual terror gradually left me. Obsessive thoughts, like 'Somebody saw me yesterday as I emptied the slops on the roof by the chimney,' or 'There's a car pulling up, I can hear the engine, it's the Gestapo, they'll be here any moment,' they went away, and I felt much, much better. I went so far as to leave the door of my cell ajar in the daytime, to get more light and air, and sometimes I went for short excursions, exploring the attic. I found a mother cat with three kittens there, and grew very fond of them.

"'The man kept looking in on me, and I looked forward to his visits. Before, I waited for the landlady, who brought my meals, for the eternally coughing landlord who brought fresh water and took the waste away, for the Gestapo with their dogs, for the nightly hours of freedom, when I could walk barefoot about the attic and the roof. Now, I waited also for him. When he came, we would sit on the pallet of straw, our faces yellow in the light of the small flame. Our words were few, our silences solemn. There were forty-nine visits. We were together, in all, only a little more than eight hours. In my attic cell I counted minutes, hours, days, weeks. I had all the time in the world to count, as I paced my cell, three steps one way, three steps back, three steps one way, three steps back. I hummed tunes, recited poetry. I danced, taking tiny steps, my mind went back to the years before the War, and I saw myself in a large ballroom. . . . Waltzes, tangos, polonaises . . . Step, bend the knee, step, arm extended, bend the knee. But the walls were in the way, my cell was too narrow. . . .

"My world was a dark, reeking hole, where beside the bench and the covered straw bag that was my bed stood a bowl that I had to use as a urinal. Where the odor of cat excrement mingled with the acrid smell of smoke escaping from a flue. Yet in this hole I suddenly realized that one could be glad of something after all, that one could miss another human being, that one could dream pleasurable dreams. . . . No, I never told him this. I meant to tell him later, after the War, but . . ."

Helena broke off and closed her eyes, then opened them and motioned with her head at the glass of cold tea which stood on her bed table.

I took the glass and, leaning over, touched her mouth with it. She drank in small sips.

"I can still drink, and I'm sure I'll eat something," she

said. "I have a few days yet. . . . Where was I? Yes, I didn't tell him, and then it was too late."

"You never saw him afterwards?" I asked, putting the glass back.

"Oh, no! I saw him." She grew animated. "He was sitting on a bench, bent over. I hardly recognized him in the daylight. He looked different, smaller, leaner. They asked me: 'Did he come to you?' I answered, 'Yes, he did.' At this he raised his head and said, 'I wanted to help her.' They asked him: 'What was the payment?' He replied, 'Jewelry, some rings.' 'I made no payment!' I shouted at the people in gowns who were sitting in judgment over him. They said to me: 'He robbed the landlord's family and other people.' "

Helena sighed. "I tried to defend him. I told them about my attic cell, where I lived through the hardest days of my life, about the cat and her kittens, about the straw and the urinal, and of the first visit he paid me there in my hole. I told them that I had looked forward to his visits, that I had missed him when he wasn't there, because he was a good person, and I was sure he would have saved my life even without the money and those rings. That's what I said, wanting it to be true. Later I visited him. . . . Would you mind straightening the pillow? That's it, a little higher . . ."

I adjusted the pillow for her and pulled my chair even closer to her bed, to hear her better, because her voice was growing weaker.

Krystyna, the aide, half-opened the door, but withdrew when she saw me.

"I visited him," Helena resumed. "I went to see him several times. We sat opposite each other, he on one side of the prison table, I on the other. The first time, I asked him,

'*Why?*' He said, 'I saved your life, that should satisfy you.' And that was all he said. But it wasn't the formal 'you' he used, it was the familiar. . . . After a few weeks I brought him an onion, some garlic, and a cake that I had baked especially for him. At that point he said: 'I had to save you, I couldn't help myself.' 'What moved you to do it?' I asked. 'Your face, your eyes, your trust in me,' he replied. 'And the rings and the money?' I asked. 'That was to be for you, for later, but nobody believes me, and I don't know if you will ever believe me.' "

Helena fell silent. She let her lids droop, and appeared to be sleeping.

"Did you believe him?" I asked in a timid whisper.

She didn't answer, but I thought she gave a nod. I got up, moved my chair away carefully and quietly left.

"Asleep?" asked Krystyna in the corridor.

"Yes," I answered. "Please don't disturb her."

"Sleep will do her good," said the aide, and disappeared into the kitchen.

Sulamith

Moishe, son of Rabbi Asher Zvi Hirtz, began his apprenticeship as a shoemaker with Abraham Mandelbaum in 1949. A year later, he fell from a ladder while hanging curtains in the apartment of his teacher and employer. The Mandelbaums hauled him to the hospital in a cart, unconscious. After three weeks Moishe returned to the workshop, but then several times fell off his stool and lost consciousness briefly. Mrs. Mandelbaum brewed herbal tea for him. "Drink," she said. "Drink, Moishele, my herbs will make you stronger, and they're good for regularity, too." The fits became rarer but did not go away altogether.

Moishe bought clear vodka in the shop across the street. He drank once a week; and as time passed, two or three times a week. One day he took from the sideboard the handbag belonging to Luba, the daughter of Sarah and Abraham Mandelbaum, and converted to vodka its entire contents, i.e., 2,400 zlotys, a wristwatch without a band, three American dollars, and a silver ring with a green stone.

The following day, Mrs. Mandelbaum told Moishe to put on his best suit, his new shoes, the ones that squeaked, and his gray hat. Moishe did so, then asked:

"Why am I dressing up? Did I forget a Jewish holiday? Or is it for Luba's wedding?"

"It is several weeks yet to the next holiday, there is no wedding, Luba is only seventeen, and you are as fit for her as an ox is to pull a coach. My Abraham will come soon, meanwhile sit down and wait."

Moishe sat on the edge of a chair. "Thank you."

Mrs. Mandelbaum sat at the table facing him and looked hard at him. He lowered his eyes.

"Why do you look away, Moishe?"

"No reason, Mrs. Mandelbaum. . . . I looked at you, now I'm looking out the window."

"Oh? And what do you see?"

"Elka Eichenberg washing her windows and singing a pretty song."

"Time to get married, Moishele. But nobody will want you."

"Why not? Because I fell from a ladder while I was hanging curtains? Or because my head spins sometimes? I have a trade, I can earn enough for myself, a wife and children . . ."

"And vodka! A Jew who drinks, Moishe, is worse than a Jew who sins. A sinner may sin once, twice, three times a year, but a drinker drinks all the time. In the last two months you were drunk seventeen times. Drunk out of your mind."

Abraham entered the room. "Up, Moishele, you are coming with me. Straighten your tie and put your hat on right," he said.

"You, Mr. Mandelbaum, are dressed up, too. . . ."

Mrs. Mandelbaum opened the wardrobe and handed her husband a navy-blue coat. "Up, Moishele, you are going with my husband."

"Where, and why?"

"We are going to Reb Chaim," Abraham said.

"But Reb Chaim lives in the old-age home."

"Yes, and I visit him once a week. Today you are coming with me."

They left together, Abraham in front, Moishe close behind him, and went to the bus stop. Before long, a bus drew up, and they got on. Abraham said nothing, but Moishe talked, gesticulating. He raised his voice and lowered it as the engine noise rose or fell.

"I was at Reb Chaim's last year. No, two years ago. Yes. It was before I fell off the ladder, in February, at Purim. So many Jews together at one table one doesn't often see. It reminded me of the little town where I was born, where I lived before the War. I remember it as I remember my father and mother, my sister and brother, my uncles, all the rest of the family, which was most of the town. Mama was a Boimelshon by birth, and we had a hundred, maybe two hundred Boimelshons. And there were twice as many Hirtzes, and as many Liperbergs—they were relatives, too—as Boimelshons, but the Rombergs outnumbered all the others. . . ."

"Enough!" Abraham said. "You are making my head spin with your uncles and cousins!"

"The Hirtzes and Boimelshons don't make my head spin. . . . I think of them wandering somewhere, from shtetl to shtetl, from village to village, on a dusty road. They are wearing long black gabardines, black hats. . . . The women are wrapped in black shawls, and the children are with the women. They walk and walk. At dusk they stop for evening prayers. They pray and pray. Then they walk again. . . ."

"And where are they going?"

"I don't know, Mr. Mandelbaum, but what I think is that they are risen from the dead and walking toward the Messiah. A good direction to go in."

"Shh. People are listening, they'll think you're not right in the head. . . ."

Reb Chaim received Abraham and Moishe in his room. Maria, the floor attendant, brought three mugs and a pot of tea from the kitchen. Reb Chaim put a basket of bread and a little china bowl full of honey on the table.

"Help yourselves, Jews," he said. "Honey never hurt anyone."

Abraham and Moishe spread honey on slices of bread, ate, and drank tea.

"Abraham, something bothers you. You squirm in your seat and don't talk."

"True, something bothers me."

"Speak."

"Reb Chaim . . . This young man here, son of Asher Zvi Hirtz, works in my shop. I take care of him, I treat him like my own, because he is the son . . ."

"Get to the point."

"Moishele drinks, and not only does he drink, he steals."

Reb Chaim raised his right hand.

"So few words, so many accusations! Enough, Abraham!"

"It is the truth."

"Moishe Hirtz is descended from a great family. Ephraim Solomon ben Aaron, the famous preacher of Lwów, was born three hundred years ago. At the annual congresses of rabbis from all over the country he preached beautiful and courageous sermons in the Lublin synagogue. And what did Ephraim Solomon ben Aaron say? He pointed the finger at the rabbis! At the faults of the rabbis! He spoke of dishonesty in their election, he spoke of the bad rearing of the young, of the improper teaching of religion. We are told that he had a beautiful, strong voice. He would begin quietly, very quietly, then build from a baritone to a mighty bass, then suddenly break off and finish his magnificent sermon almost in a whisper. Ephraim Solomon wrote a commentary to the Five Books of Moses. . . . Reb Nathan in Łęczyca permitted me to read this commentary when I was sixteen. Yes, when I was sixteen."

"But what does that have to do with my business, Reb Chaim?" asked Abraham Mandelbaum.

"Your apprentice, Moishe ben Asher Zvi, is descended from the family of the preacher Ephraim Solomon ben Aaron of Lwów."

"I didn't know that."

"Now you know, and thank the Lord for bestowing such an apprentice on you."

"Now I know."

Moishe sat motionless. He wasn't listening, he was thinking of Elka Eichenberg.

She had said to him: "Come when it gets dark. Take off your shoes at the door, give two knocks, then three, then another two." And he had taken off his shoes and knocked. "Zelig's asleep in the other room," she whispered. "I gave him a sleeping pill. He's been taking sleeping pills for two weeks. The doctor made out a prescription yesterday for another twenty-five. So you can come to me twenty-five times.

I'll teach you what to do on your wedding night. Luba won't teach you anything, and anyway she won't let a simple shoemaker touch her. She's an intellectual, finished high school, and even thinks they'll accept her in the university. . . ."

"They have accepted her," Moishe said, sitting on the bed as Elka instructed him.

"She'll become an engineer," Elka sighed, pulling off her skirt. "Undo the buttons of my camisole, Moishele. Don't pull, do it gently, and then you can kiss the back of my neck. There, lower down. Still lower. I like the back of my neck kissed. I'm clean, I took a special bath." Moishe kissed the back of her neck, then turned her around, embraced her, and then they were lying together on the feather bed.

In the morning Moishe said, "I'd like to do this with Luba. She is so beautiful."

Elka laughed. "Oh, Moishele, Luba is not for you. Zelig's hard life will soon be over. The doctors give him two, three months. I've worked it all out. You'll marry me when I'm free. . . . Luba is not for you."

"I saw her," said Moishe, "when she walked in the May Day parade. She wore a white shirt and a red tie and was the best-looking girl there. She's an activist, she makes speeches at meetings, she doesn't believe in God. . . . The Mandelbaums had a quarrel about that. Mrs. Mandelbaum sides with her daughter."

"So I'll buy a red tie," Elka said. "And the white shirt is no problem, I have four white shirts. I've saved up a little, too, we can open a shop of our own. You'll repair shoes, and I'll make smart dresses."

"It wouldn't be right to compete with Mr. Mandelbaum. He's my teacher. I was in the camp with his son Elias. Elias went up the chimney, in smoke. Whenever I see a chimney I think of Elias. In their bedroom, over the night table, is a photograph of him as a soldier. I wouldn't mind being a soldier."

Elka drew Moishe close to her. "My soldier boy," she whispered. She threw the mattress on the floor, pushed Moishe onto it, and slid down after him, giggling. He embraced her as if he had Luba in his arms. "Luba, Luba," he murmured, closing his eyes.

"Moishe ben Asher Zvi! Wake up! Do you hear me?"

Moishe started, got up from the chair.

"Yes, Reb Chaim."

"Go out into the hall, my boy, sit down in the chair by the window, and wait for Mr. Mandelbaum."

Moishe did as he was told.

"Now that your apprentice is out of the room, I will tell you something very important," Reb Chaim said to Abraham Mandelbaum. "But first let me ask you to check the ladder that Moishe fell from. It may have been defective. Also, Sarah, your wife, will have to be taught how to take care of a good apprentice. Moishe needs treatment. Buy wormwood greens, Abraham, and add them to the vodka. After two or three times Moishe will lose his taste for alcohol."

"I don't know that my Sarah will want to take the trouble. In her opinion Moishe should simply stop drinking."

"He won't stop, Abraham, he won't stop."

"Reb Chaim, there is another thing . . ."

"I'm listening."

"Moishele is after my Luba. . . . With Luba, too, I have troubles. I fear that with her the line of honest and God-fearing Mandelbaums will come to an end. It is no longer a matter of kosher food or keeping the Sabbath, it's worse. She's turning away from us, she's ashamed of her father and mother. She does well at school, too well, if you ask me. . . . She treats me like a stranger, she says God is an invention of the capitalists and imperialists, of rabbis and clergymen of other faiths. She quotes Marx, dresses and behaves as no Mandelbaum should. My wife sees nothing wrong in this, but I see great unhappiness ahead for Luba and ourselves!"

"Yes, I understand. . . . A father not up to raising a daughter . . . You are not raising her properly. Perhaps you don't know how, or haven't got the energy to talk with her. Or you are afraid and don't know what to say. . . . Ephraim Solomon ben Aaron of Lwów would have answered you as follows: 'Abraham, you said your Luba quotes Marx. But perhaps she is right to quote Marx to you, because you are stingy, very stingy, coming here to complain about an apprentice to whom you owe a lot of money. He works and gets only his breakfast, lunch, and supper . . . ' "

"And lodging, and laundry . . ."

"Don't interrupt, you are talking with Ephraim Solomon ben Aaron of Lwów, not with an ordinary Jew named Chaim. . . . Don't be surprised that your daughter, seeing injustice in your house, looks for justice elsewhere. But even if you see the light and change completely, that doesn't mean your daughter will burst into tears, kiss her father's hand, and renounce Marx. The world has changed since the destruction of Jerusalem, and it has changed even more since the destruction of Warsaw and of our shtetl! No, my friend, you can't forbid your daughter to think. But you can influence her actions. If she stays honest and upholds the traditions of our fathers, she will remain your Luba. . . . But that is a big if. My advice is this: Let Moishe ben Asher Zvi marry Luba Mandelbaum."

"Reb Chaim!"

"I didn't say she has to. . . . Have a talk with your daughter, tell her that Moishe needs special care, that only she can help him. . . . Buy her an expensive present, and buy your apprentice something, too, and let him buy her something. Spend a little. Starting today, you, Abraham Mandelbaum, are no longer a tightwad, but a good, sober, honest Jew."

"I'll try . . ."

"If we don't change your daughter, at least we will change you. Do you understand what Ephraim Solomon ben Aaron of Lwów has been saying to you?"

"Yes, I understand."

Meanwhile, in the hallway, Moishe sat, his eyes closed, seeing Luba in her white shirt and red tie. She came and went in his vision, and finally gave way to Elka in a nightgown. Elka, smiling, beckoned to him. Moishe opened his eyes. Before him stood Rivka.

"Sleeping?" she asked in a low voice.

"No, I saw Luba, then Elka, and now I see you."

"I dreamt of you last night," said Rivka. "No, it wasn't a dream. You stood in the doorway. I saw you!" She turned away and slipped into her room.

Moishe meant to follow her but heard Mr. Mandelbaum's voice behind him.

"We are going, Moishe. Was that Rivka? Do you like her?"

"Luba is prettier."

"Luba is not for you."

"I know, Mr. Mandelbaum. That is why she is in my thoughts."

That night Moishe could not sleep. He saw Luba in bed next to him. "Take off your shirt and the red tie," he said. With a smile she replied, "I can't, I'm off to meet my fiancé." "No!" Moishe shouted and punched her in the face, first the right cheek, then the left cheek. She laughed, and he heard that laughter as he groped his way down the stairs and into the dark street.

On a stone bench, under an unlit streetlamp, he sat and soliloquized. "Ah, Mrs. Mandelbaum, why did you take my bottle? It had more than a quarter liter of vodka in it, which you like to call schnapps. And now I suffer, while you sleep like a baby at Mr. Mandelbaum's side, and he even puts his arms around you and murmurs something. Even in the kitchen I can hear him, although you keep the door closed.

"What harm did I do, Mrs. Mandelbaum? What does the world have against me? My father was a rabbi, pious, wise, and learned, but he received a death sentence from the Almighty. They cut off his beard with a knife, then pulled out his *peyis* and ordered him to sing, but he didn't, he wouldn't say Heil Hitler either, and his blood trickled down my head, throat, down to my stomach and legs, and made the cold ground wet. I was barefoot on that ground where Mother used to plant flowers and radishes, and now you take my bottle away. Why did you do that? Luba, your dear daughter, won't look at me, while I would lay down my life for her."

He got up, crossed the street, entered the lighted gateway, climbed the stairs to the fifth floor, and knocked at the door.

"Is that you?" Elka asked. "But I can't today, I told you, and anyway it's late. Go, Moishele. Come in a few days. Friday, Saturday . . ."

"Let me in, Luba."

"I am not Luba. What's the matter with you?" And she slammed the door.

He sat on the stairs and rested his head against the wall.

"Father taught me that the Fair One in the Song of Songs was really Israel. I don't know, Father, if your Rabbi Akiba was right. To me the Fair One is Luba, Sulamith is Luba. . . . But I can't remember the song! Luba's laughter gets in the way."

He went back to the door and knocked, and knocked again. Only after he pounded the door with his fist several times did Elka open it. He pushed her aside and ran into the room.

"Where is he?" Moishe shouted. "The fiancé!" In the darkness he saw a figure lying on the bed, hurled himself at it, pulled the sheet away, seized the man by the throat. "No more fiancé for you! I will be the fiancé!"

Elka lit the candle on the table, sat down in a chair, and said: "My poor Moishele. Zelig died this afternoon. Look closely, he is yellow and cold."

Moishe turned to Elka.

"Elka, what harm did I do to the world? What does the world have against me? My father was a good rabbi, his name was Asher Zvi, everyone knew him. Tell me, Elka, what does God have against me?"

"I don't know," she said.

Diamond or Glass

Schmul Rautman, alias Rodakowski, alias Karmiński, survived the Occupation with "Aryan" papers as Szymon Stefan Rodakowski, and after 1943 as Szymon Stefan Karmiński. At the job they called him Radowski, then Rautman, and for the past two years Mr. Piłsudski, the latter because the resident nurse talked him into growing a beautiful silver-gray mustache on the model of the prewar marshal of Poland.

Mr. Rautman tried to convince the doctors, nurses, orderlies, and himself that he had throat cancer. The tests contradicted this, but he did not care. At each examination he brought up his imaginary affliction. Several times a day he looked at his throat. He would stand before the bathroom mirror or the mirror in his room, or even the mirror in the lobby, open his mouth, and, raising and lowering his head, say, "Aaaah!"

He lived alone but liked company. Julian and Leizor would sometimes drop by, or old David, or restless Feivel with calm

Rose, or sometimes nosy Malka or one-legged Rivka, but most frequently Abraham Roman Miedow.

The two of them, Mr. Rautman and Mr. Miedow, were sitting at the table. Mr. Rautman folded his hands over his potbelly, but Mr. Miedow's hands fidgeted on the table, sometimes upsetting an ashtray or a little vase.

"Stop that," Mr. Rautman finally said. "With your dirty hands you'll knock over my sugar bowl, and spilled salt means a quarrel in the house."

"Salt in a sugar bowl?" Mr. Miedow asked incredulously.

"Yes, and in the saltshaker I have pepper. Does that surprise you?"

"No, nothing surprises me," Mr. Miedow assured him. He quickly added: "My hands are not dirty, I keep them scrupulously clean, washing before every meal and after going to the toilet, as halakhah requires."

"What do *you* know of halakhah?"

Mr. Miedow puffed, indignant. "My grandfather was a shamus in the synagogue."

"And your father?" asked Mr. Rautman.

"So he fled to the city with my mother and they ate pork. They had to stay alive, after all. In wartime we didn't keep kosher. Anyway, I resent your insinuation about my family."

"Pish tush," Mr. Rautman said with a smile. "We are both not getting any younger. Let's not fight. But it's important now for us to tell the truth of our lives. We must shed our secrets, they are burdens . . . in our breasts, in our heads. . . . Telling them, we reduce their weight, we feel lighter, more at peace with ourselves."

"A confession," said Mr. Miedow.

"A cleaning of the heart."

"Of garbage?"

"No, not of garbage. . . ." Mr. Rautman reflected, then said: "Our secrets aren't garbage but precious stones, the diamonds of life. We exchange diamonds with each other. I give you a diamond, you give me a diamond."

Mr. Miedow shook his head. "Mine are not all diamonds. Some are only glass."

"That depends on one's point of view."

"Possibly," said Mr. Miedow doubtfully. "But a diamond is a diamond, and glass is glass, and there is nothing you can do about that. I will tell you a story, and, when I'm done, you say whether it is diamond or glass. All right?"

"All right," said Mr. Rautman.

Mr. Miedow pushed himself away from the table, crossed his legs, took off his glasses, rubbed the lenses with his thumbs, folded the glasses, and put them into a side pocket of his coat. With a sigh he began his narrative.

"My name is Abraham, but there was a time, I'll tell you about that in a minute, when I was called Roman, Romanek, Romeczek. I was in the military, an NCO, with a fitted uniform and boots that gleamed like a dog's nose after it sniffs a side of bacon. I saw some fighting, but I'll say nothing about that here. Perhaps another time. The War came to an end, and I decided to return to the little town where I was born. But what did the good Lord do? He had me step into a restaurant for a good civilian meal and meet a beautiful waitress. The waitress served me *shchi,* and to this day I don't know if it was the Lord's doing, too, or simply my future wife's, but she stumbled, and the *shchi* went all over my coat, tie, and trousers. And because of the *shchi* I found myself, next thing, at the Registrar's office saying yes. And she said yes, and we were a married couple. . . . Mr. Rautman, you can't imagine how beautiful she was! I myself was amazed that I had such a beauty for a wife and that I could actually go to bed with her. Only then did I understand why my private, Yegor Arbunov, blew his brains out when he learned that his fiancée had married an invalid, a major, who returned from the War earlier than he did. And only then did I understand why another of my soldiers, Felek Nurek, crawled out of the trench and waited for a German sniper to pick him off, because he had received a letter from his mother telling him that his Krysia had been hanged in the market square by the Nazis."

"And the sniper killed him?" asked Mr. Rautman.

"No."

"Well, that was lucky."

"Yes, lucky." Mr. Miedow put his palms down on the tablecloth. "I had to punch Felek in the mouth for leaving the trench without an order, but he returned the favor later, after the War. I'll get to that, too. . . . Anyway, getting back to my beautiful wife and our going to bed, and what came of it. Quite a lot did. . . . As I told you, she was so pretty, so graceful, she didn't even have to stand in line for groceries or theater tickets. And the lines in the forties were long."

"So they were, I remember," Mr. Rautman said.

"My wife would stand near some man and smile, showing her shining white teeth and deep brown eyes, and say, 'I was ahead of you in line, wasn't I?' "

"And the man would always say she was," suggested Mr. Rautman.

"Every time." Mr. Miedow nodded and went on with his

story. "My wife said to me one day: 'Starting today, your name is not Abraham Miedow, but Roman Miedow, Romanek, Romeczek. And I am Małgorzata, Małgosia, Maga.' We were starting a new life, she explained, because she had found a job in a different restaurant—as the vocalist in a musical group called Our Aces. 'Well,' I thought to myself, 'good-bye Abraham, hello Roman.' It also occurred to me that this meant trouble, because if a man has a beautiful wife, he needs to hide her, and here she would be working in a place filled with prime specimens of manhood. . . . In a word, I became jealous. Whoever smiled at her or said something nice, I suspected. I suspected the whole musical ensemble, the waiters, the manager, the two cloakroom attendants, the cook. That was not at all funny, Mr. Rautman, it was unbearable! I followed her more than once, but could prove nothing against her. We were in each other's company day and night. Why day and night, you ask? Because we worked in the same restaurant. I was one of the waiters, and she, as I told you, sang."

"I had no idea that you were a waiter, no idea!" Mr. Rautman said, surprised.

"Well, now you know, Mr. Rautman, and I must tell you that I am not ashamed of it. I learned to see people in a new and interesting way. Let me explain: a cabaret is a place where people eat, drink, dance, flirt a little, listen to music, and exchange a little gossip. They get into a different mood—they escape the daily grind for an hour or two. The waiter is the servant, the patron the master. And the cook is a servant, too, and the cloakroom attendant, and the musician, singer, barmaid, maître d' and busboy, they're all at the patron's beck and call. Welcome! Step right in, sir. An honor and a pleasure! . . . I have seen them all exhausted: the violinist, the busboy, the saxophonist, the cook, the singer bathed in sweat, the spent look of the maître d'. A cabaret is where dreams are fulfilled—the dreams of last week, last month, last year. For money, a hundred zlotys, a thousand, we buy music, a Swiss steak, a tango on the dance floor, a shot of vodka, a smile from the waitress, a waiter's bow, and tea with lemon, or a soda, or champagne. Here people get acquainted, drink and dance together, quarrel sometimes, even fight. Deals are made, agreements entered into, appointments kept. . . . I haven't told you anything you didn't know, have I? I simply wanted you to grasp the situation.

"My uncle, you know, my mother's brother, Jacob, had an inn. All kinds of people congregated there, Jews, Byelorussians, Poles, Gypsies, and one time even some Tatar stopped in with his little son. The guests were seated at a long table and ate together. There were three smaller tables, too, but they were set only on holidays or for special guests. Jacob used to say: 'I give people what they need most at the moment. I take care of them. In the winter they need warmth, so I give them warmth, I give them hot tea from the samovar. In the summer they want to cool off, so I cool them off and give them cold bread kvass. They want to sleep? Here, a nice clean, warm feather bed and a down comforter. They want a good time? Here, a pint of beer, some vodka, and if a man wants to have a little cry over his booze, that's his business, he's paid his money. And even if he hasn't paid and still wants to cry over his booze, his credit is always good with me, as mine is with the Lord. How many times have I had things on credit from the Lord! Once, during the pogrom in the Ukraine before the Revolution. Another time, when I fell into a hole in the ice and caught pneumonia. And again, when I got the Spanish flu. If the Almighty grants me credit, why shouldn't I do the same for others?' No, Uncle Jacob was no tightwad. On my thirteenth birthday, for my bar mitzvah, he gave me a big pocket watch. I don't have it anymore, and Uncle Jacob is no longer among the living."

"His credit with the Lord ran out," said Mr. Rautman.

"Sometimes," Mr. Miedow went on, "when I remember my childhood, I start talking with a Jewish accent, like dear Uncle Jacob. The past is over and done with, and yet somehow . . . Anyway, my work in the restaurant with the nightclub and bar was tiring but interesting. Sometimes poetic types from distant cities visited us, wearing black cloaks, and our place attracted painters, writers, students. Some wrote verses, clever things, on their paper napkins, and I held on to those for a long time. Ah, Mr. Rautman, the things I saw and heard there . . . Anyway, it was spring, May or late April, when one of the patrons insisted I down a tumbler of vodka with him. The man was a captain with tons of medals on his uniform, and he had clearly seen action, because his forehead was scarred and his left ear was gone except for a small lump of flesh. It would have been a sin to refuse to drink with such a man. We put away perhaps half a bottle. When I got back to the kitchen, I naturally didn't feel well. The boss and one of the waitresses, Ula, dragged me into a little room next door and deposited me on a couch, where I went to sleep."

"Vodka will do that," observed Mr. Rautman.

"Well, yes. Anyway, I woke up around midnight and saw that Ula was asleep in an armchair. She woke up too, or perhaps she hadn't been asleep but was only watching over me. I don't know. She said to me: 'Your little wife has gone off with the one-eared captain, she likes medals.' I leaped for the door, but it was locked. I begged for the key, but Ula wouldn't let me have it, she laughed and made fun of me. My head throbbed, I felt awful, I was still drunk. Then Ula cursed my wife, calling her all sorts of names. She gave me some curdled milk and told me to go back to sleep. When I woke up the second time that night, Ula was lying beside me. And in bed, Mr. Rautman, it turned out that she was no worse than my wife! In the morning I got dressed, unlocked the door, and left the little room. I wanted a drink, but as I went to the bar, I heard loud snoring. It was the one-eared captain, peacefully asleep on a table at the end of the room."

"I don't understand."

"Well, I put two and two together. Yes, there it was, Mr. Rautman, I had betrayed my beautiful wife, not she me. And unfortunately she found out within a few hours. To make matters worse, some helpful person made it his business to tell her that Ula and I had been going at it for months. . . . There was a scene, and we separated. I began to drink. No, I didn't become an alcoholic. . . . I drank because I was miserable. I changed restaurants, but my new job didn't last. A drunk waiter doesn't belong in a respectable establishment.

"One day, at a bus stop, I met a soldier from my outfit, Felek Nurek. Felek was passing through Warsaw on reassignment, so I invited him to my place. He had supper with me and was on the point of leaving, in a hurry to catch a train, when I told him: 'Felek, I am just like you that time, climbing out of the trench and waiting for a sniper to pick me off.' Whereupon he said: 'I'll punch you in the mouth if you leave the trench without orders,' and he stayed with me for two days, because I was depressed. We talked about the War and our buddies, those who survived and those who didn't make it. . . . Yes, Mr. Rautman, shared memories, in those two days, helped me, helped me a lot."

"Nowadays," Mr. Rautman said, nodding, "they call that psychotherapy."

"Yes, I'm a different person now, I've changed, and so, I'm sure, have you. Warsaw has changed, we've all changed. I live now with my blind Marianka, who is the very opposite of my former wife. I've gone from one extreme to the other. Marianka has swollen legs, fingers twisted by arthritis, and a hernia from abdominal surgery, but she belongs to me. She's a wise woman. Agreed, there's no beauty in the bed, no body smooth as softest silk. . . . Where do I come up with smooth as softest silk, you ask? From a poem on a paper napkin, written for me by a poet I gave ten zlotys to for cab fare. A collector's item, that napkin. I still have it. I'll show it to you someday. But now Marianka . . . she needs me. We respect each other. We've been living together for eight years and never had a quarrel. 'I'd still be an old maid if it wasn't for you,' she always tells me. 'I'd be thinking of poisoning or hanging myself. My schoolmates, cousins, best friends all got married, and I stayed single. And then, when I was a cripple and sick besides, and lost all hope, my man, my own man, showed up.' And she's educated—she comes from a professor's family, a professor of Greek and Latin, so compared to her I'm a boor, an ignoramus. And now, Mr. Rautman, choose where in all this lies the precious diamond, and where the cheap glass."

Mr. Rautman laughed. "The important thing is that you are now lighter for your story."

"True, I am lighter," said Mr. Miedow, and rose from his

chair. "If you don't mind, I have to go now. She is probably worrying about my being away so long."

"I understand, I understand perfectly," said Mr. Rautman, seeing his guest to the door.

Three Left

On April 5, 1945, Michael Kramer returned from the camp to his hometown, Soligród. The sections in which the Jews had lived were completely destroyed; their houses and barns had been burned down by the Nazis. All that remained was a church, a two-story building where the town authorities had their offices, the marketplace, the hospital, and a few dozen battered houses in the southern part of the town.

On August 2, 1942, Jacob Dawidowicz, four years old, was hidden by Maria Liwiec of Zagródek—under a barn.

Mirele Samborowicz and three girlfriends fled Soligród just before the liquidation of the town's Jews in the middle of August 1942. The girls lived in the forest, but after three weeks the military police discovered their shelter and marched them to the railroad station, where they were put on a train, already filled with Jews, headed for Treblinka. Mirele escaped from the transport and returned to the forest.

Michael

When I returned, I found our little town vacant. The houses were not there, the streets were not there, and the people were missing. Walking, I saw the absence of a scrawny goat, of an old horse, of flowers, of the sky I remembered. I passed familiar places that no longer existed, a church, a town hall, a park bench. On Grobelna Street was the synagogue, gone, existing for me alone, like our house, which was gone, too.

On the road to the village of Zagródek I saw myself: sitting on a big rock and playing with five pebbles, throwing them in the air and catching them. Nearby, grazing, stood a russet cow, and a bay horse with its legs hobbled, so instead of walking, it made strange little hops, throwing its head to the left and the right. Over each animal was a swarm of flies, and occasionally a swallow swooped across, barely missing the horse's head. The cow belonged to Big Golda, and the horse to the *pachter,* the Jewish tenant farmer, David Dawidowicz, whose son, Jacob Dawidowicz, was born in a church.

Here is how it happened. Mrs. Dawidowicz had gone to the market on Friday, and in the course of fierce haggling over a hen went into labor. So she paid what the peasant woman demanded, clapped the hen under her arm, and, groaning with pain, made for home. Suddenly there was lightning, thunder, and it started pouring. Mrs. Dawidowicz wanted to run but couldn't. The hen struggled under her arm, the rain came down in buckets, and there was more lightning. She called loudly on the Almighty, her mother, her husband, her mother-in-law, her sisters-in-law Sheyndla and Sura, and her brothers Abram and Yankel, but only the peasant woman heard her, and she paid little attention. But when Mrs. Dawidowicz slipped and fell in a mud puddle right in front of the church and the hen broke loose from her hands, the peasant woman realized that something was wrong. She came running, pulled Mrs. Dawidowicz from the mud, and helped her, almost unconscious, into the church, where a new Dawidowicz of the male gender promptly entered the world, Jacob.

Before his son's circumcision, Mr. Dawidowicz betook himself to the rabbi to ask if the child's non-Jewish birth presented a problem. The wise rabbi spoke as follows: "Better the child should be born in the church than in the mud. The church is visited from time to time by the Lord God Himself (for He is not, as you and I both know, always present in the synagogue). So you must thank the priest." "And how am I to thank the priest?" asked David Dawidowicz. "Bring him the hen which your Dvoira bought from the peasant woman," suggested the rabbi. "But the hen escaped!" said David Dawidowicz. "In that case, give the priest another hen, but buy it from the same peasant woman, and be sure not to haggle over the price." "But why from the same peasant woman, and why pay her whatever she asks?" asked David Dawidowicz. "In this way," said the rabbi, "you will reward her for the help she gave your wife and little son in the rain and lightning."

Down the road from Zagródek came a girl, and behind her a large white dog. "Are you waiting here for somebody?" she asked me. "Yes, I am," I said. The dog barked a little, then was silent. "I am waiting, too," she said. We sat in the grass, and the dog sat beside us. I looked closely at the girl. She was about thirteen and had a sad face. "My stepfather hasn't come back," she said after a while. "They say he stayed *there*"—she waved her hand at the forest beyond the river—"but Mother doesn't believe it. Come, maybe you can convince her." "Why me of all people?" I asked. "You're from *there,*" she said.

I followed her and the dog to a hut, where I found a young woman with gray hair. "There are few of us left," she said. This was the same peasant woman who had delivered Jacob Dawidowicz in the church that Friday of the great thunderstorm. "The boy's alive, he's my godson," she said. "But he's always afraid."

Little Jacob sat hunched up and refused to come out of his hiding place under a corn crib. I asked him why. He didn't answer. How long, I asked him, was he going to stay with the woman? "She saved my life," he said. "And Józia saved me, too, by saying nothing. She kept silent for two years, even though she's still a child." "You're a child yourself," I told him. He answered, "The policeman questioned her and patted her head, then shouted at her and hit her. But she didn't tell. She will always be my sister."

I went back into the yard. The girl sat on the stump of a tree, stroking the white dog. Her mother was sitting at the door. I sat down on the ground nearby.

"Mrs. Dawidowicz came by early that morning," she told me. "I was lighting the stove. She warmed her swollen hands at the fire. I gave her something to eat. Then she said: 'You brought my boy into the world, and now he will perish. Won't you take pity on him?' That's what she said, and I knew at once that the child would be mine. I asked where he was. 'Waiting for you,' she said, 'in the burnt-out blacksmith's shop, in the right-hand corner. I covered him with rags and straw. You'll find him.' At night I stole across the bog and the thicket and went along the river. I found him. He was such a weak little thing. When I carried him back, Mrs. Dawidowicz was gone. I took the rags off my baby, bathed him, and hid him under the stall. I found this on him." She held out her hand, and I saw on her palm a tiny oblong wooden box. I opened it and saw a mezuzah. Inside it there was a closely inscribed piece of parchment.

"Do you know what it says?" she asked. I nodded. "Tell me, then. Read it to me. Jacob would like to hear it, too. I'll bring him. I'm sure he'll come out to hear it. He's always wanted to know what it said." And she brought Jacob out. He blinked in the sun and began coughing. She gave him a mug of water and sat him down next to her.

I translated the parchment for them.

"Again, about the grain, the earth, and the cattle," she said.

" 'Then He will let down the rain upon the land in proper season, autumn and spring,' " I read slowly, reflecting on each word. " 'And thou wilt gather thy grain, thy grape must, and thine oil. And I will send grass in thy fields for thy cattle, and thou mayest eat and be full.' "

"Those are good prophecies," she said. "I didn't know I was keeping something like that in my house. It will bring good luck."

I asked what happened to Big Golda.

"Are you her son?" The young girl looked up.

"No. I saw her cow in the meadow."

"What happened to Big Golda is what happened to all the

Goldas, Moishes, and Abrahams," the woman answered. "And the cow is not the same cow."

"And the horse? Mr. Dawidowicz had a horse like that, didn't he?"

She sighed. "The horse and the cow were brought here by our soldiers. They took them from the Nazis."

But I insisted. "It's Big Golda's cow and it's Mr. Dawidowicz's horse."

"No," she said, growing impatient, "they were eaten, and long ago, right at the beginning of the Occupation. I bought a piece of the horsemeat myself. A whole week we filled our bellies on that. I remember."

There was a silence. The dog made the rounds of the yard and returned to the girl.

"What will you do now?" the girl asked me.

"I don't know," I said.

"You'll get married."

"Someday, maybe . . ."

"I know someone," she said. "She will be your wife."

"You're talking nonsense," the mother scolded.

"It's the truth," the girl insisted. "A young woman came back, too. I saw her, she lives with the people from Warsaw, behind the ruins of the warden's house."

"From Warsaw?" I marveled. "What kind of people from Warsaw are here?"

"The Topolewiczes. In nineteen-forty they stopped at Aniela's, the widow of Andrzej Borodzik. Then Aniela died, and they sort of settled in the house," explained the mother. "But I didn't know that anyone had come to stay with them."

"Come, I'll show you," said the girl, getting up. The dog

got up, too, and wagged his bushy tail. "Atlas will go with us, won't you, Atlas?"

We walked down a wide village road. On both sides stood gutted houses, stables, sties. In the yards lay empty carts, hay wagons, tables, chairs, and cupboards toppled and smashed. Half-buried in the mud were pots, kettles large and small, ripped-open feather beds and pillows. The wind was carrying away scraps of fabric.

As we jumped over puddles, the girl kept alerting me: "Watch out—water!" "Watch out—mud!" The dog chased swallows that flew past almost at ground level, or he went exploring into abandoned yards. The girl would call him back, but he only showed himself for a moment, then vanished again. Finally she gave a long whistle. Atlas leaped out of a roadside ditch and with his head low came to the girl. She patted his rump, and he lay down. "Good Atlas, good dog," she said tenderly. "You stay with us."

"Are you afraid?" I asked.

"People say the ghosts of murdered Jews roam here."

"Those are good ghosts," I told her. "I would like to talk to them. But I don't know if they will talk to me. Don't be afraid, little one. There is nothing to be afraid of." We walked on in silence.

Suddenly she pointed to a little hut at the far end of a yard. We went up to the gate. Two black mongrels started baying. Atlas growled, his mane bristling. A woman appeared in the doorway.

"Good morning, ma'am!" the girl called to her. "It's me, Józia Liwiec!"

"And you?" asked the woman, addressing me. "What brings you here?"

"He's our guest," the girl said. "He wants to meet your guest."

"I have no guests," the woman said, and turned away.

"Please," I said. "I used to live in the town. I'm looking for relatives. Perhaps one of them has survived . . . I had a sister!"

"You don't need to shout." She made the dogs stop barking. "People might hear. Come in."

"What if they do?" I asked in the doorway.

She didn't answer, only showed us to places at a table. We sat down. Atlas went under the table and growled from time to time. Mrs. Topolewicz brought two mugs full of milk, set them before us, and took a seat.

"So you're from the town?" she asked.

"Yes," I said, "but it's empty."

"People are returning."

"The Jews are not returning."

"I know," she said. "I'm sorry. But the town has to live."

Hearing movement behind me, I turned. "Mirele!" I exclaimed. "Is it you?"

She sat down with us. "I waited such a long time, but nobody came," she said in a low voice. "I told myself to be patient. What is there left for us but to wait?"

"But Mirele, aren't you glad to see me?"

"Yes, though our families were not on the best of terms. . . ."

"That was ages ago, before the War."

"Before the War . . . My people were observant, yours were not. You went to high school, I studied at home. It would be nice if we could still be enemies. Your father against my father, your mother against my mother. Remember how they fought at the market or in Mr. Majerowicz's shop? One would yank a cheap black-and-red checkered kerchief out of the other's hand, or a swatch of silk, or a pair of cotton stockings. 'I was here first,' your mother would shout. 'Are you crazy, I was ahead of you,' my mother would shout. And Mr. Majerowicz would wait patiently, then take an identical pair of cotton stockings off a shelf, or a swatch of silk, or a black-and-red checkered kerchief, and say in his rumbling voice: 'So what's to quarrel about? I have any number you want of this item. Fifty kerchiefs you want? Here, fifty kerchiefs. A hundred meters of silk? A hundred meters of silk it is. And stockings, please. I have thirty-five pair of the finest quality cotton in different colors and sizes.'

"And our mothers would glare at Mr. Majerowicz, and leave the shop without buying anything. Lord, what splendid fights they had, and what splendid apologies, and then more fights . . ." Mirele did not finish. After a moment, she added in a whisper, "I've been waiting, waiting . . ."

"It's good that you came here," Mrs. Topolewicz said and put a third mug of milk in front of Mirele.

Mirele

Walking through the forest, I recognized my trees, the three talking firs that seemed to grow from a single trunk, they stood so close to one another. I remembered, from my early childhood, Mr. Borodzik's tale about the three sisters bewitched into three fir trees, and the tale of the spruce that bent over during storms to protect the little sapling that grew next to it, and how, years later, the sapling outgrew and then protected the spruce. Both perished in the first days of the Occupation. The Nazis cut them down on the same day, at the same hour.

I took the path my mother used to take when we visited the Borodziks. It was during the Occupation, when one had to hide from the Germans. Sometimes we would stay all night with the Borodziks and sneak back home before dawn, never sure if the German soldiers were still in the town or had left.

I walked barefoot. The grass and moss cooled my feet. I tilted my head back and watched the wind sweeping through the treetops. Little white and gray clouds traveled rapidly across the sky, now brightening, now darkening the earth. I felt good, felt that there was only the forest, the sky, and the cool grass and moss underfoot. I hopped on one foot like a child playing hopscotch, and hummed a tune of my own invention. I spun, I skipped. Never had I felt so good. And yet a moment ago I had been afraid, afraid of the rustle of the branches and of the silence of the forest.

A woodpecker rapped on a tree once, twice, a hundred times, greeting me with his knock-knock-knock, keeping me company all the way to Zagródek.

The Borodzik house was unharmed. I hesitated, not knowing whom I might find there. Suddenly the head of a black dog showed between the rails of the gate. He gave a hoarse bark, and a second dog barked from inside the yard. The Borodziks had had a small ginger mongrel, but here were two big black ones, and fierce, too. The house must have been taken over by someone else.

A woman approached the gate. She wore a wide black skirt, a white short-sleeved blouse, and a black bow in her dark-blonde hair. "Are you looking for somebody?" she asked.

"The Borodziks," I said, and was about to turn away, but she opened the gate wide and invited me in.

The kitchen smelled of baked bread as always, and of cabbage and herbs. Potatoes were boiling in a pot. I felt very hungry. "Bronka Borodzik died a year ago," said the lady. "We are the Topolewiczes. My husband was a cousin of Bronka's on her paternal uncle's side. Bronka often spoke to us about a girl named Mila."

"That's me, but at home I'm Mirele," I said, and saw a smile on her lips and a kind look.

Mr. Topolewicz's head appeared in the window, then he entered. A tall, redheaded man with large blue eyes, he sat down at the table and said, "We have a guest, I see. We've had many guests here, but you're special. Let's have something good to eat, wife."

I cringed, afraid of him, afraid of his red hair and blue eyes, afraid even when he spoke and smiled. But finally I looked up at him, took in his face, the shock of hair that fell over his forehead, the palm held out toward his wife. I said to myself, then, that it would be good if this burly man put his hand on my cheek, if he took me in his arms and hugged me. I half-closed my eyes and despite myself said, aloud, "No!" But they paid no attention to me, engaged in a conversation I couldn't hear.

I stayed with them. "Rest, and then we'll see," they said. I rested. I roamed the house, grew accustomed to furniture, to white sheets on the bed, to small rooms. Sometimes I felt stifled. At first I shied away from the bathtub, but later I took several baths a day. I washed for no reason. I would pour water into the bowl, stare into the clear liquid, then wash my hands. I would fall asleep in the middle of the day, wake up at night, and not know where I was. Sometimes I helped Mrs. Topolewicz in the kitchen or the yard. I fed the chickens and the geese, weeded in the garden, but she wouldn't allow me to do real work. "Plenty of time for that," she would say. "You'll have all the work you want."

They didn't ask to hear about my wanderings through the forests and swamps of the Podlasie country, about the crowds of exhausted people who, wanting to live, fed on berries, roots, dead birds. About the freight car that stank of feces, urine, sweat, and chlorine, and the rotting corpse of a girl. About the meadow by the railroad tracks, where with others I waited five days and nights in mud and rain, and was beaten, spat upon, killed. I didn't want to talk, either, but images of that time would appear suddenly, unexpectedly, at lunch, while talking with Mrs. Topolewicz about completely different things, or by the chicken coop while I was throwing grain to the hens. And then it would seem to me that I was back there, with Itka and Chanusia in the forest, or later with Itka and without Chanusia on the ice and snow of the marshes.

One day, when Mr. and Mrs. Topolewicz went out, I entered their bedroom and sat on their bed. Suddenly one of the black dogs, Bass, came in, wagging his tail, and lay down on the floor by my bare feet. When I stroked the dog's smooth fur with my feet, he raised his head and looked attentively at me. "You have lovely brown eyes," I whispered, "and a wet nose. You're the most beautiful dog in the world. Mirele loves you very, very much. She's glad you don't know what a ghetto is. What the basement of a police station is. Or a heap of rotten hay in December, or a leaky dugout in November."

So I talked with Bass, and he liked hearing me, and I was

going to tell him about my waiting and that I still didn't know what or who I was waiting for but that I would be patient—when I heard the gate squeak. Bass jumped up and started barking, and I ran out of the room and hid in the closet. Mr. and Mrs. Topolewicz came back, but I sat crouched in the closet, feeling I had betrayed them.

Bass became my friend. I had long talks with him, and was sure he understood me, he alone.

The next day, at lunch, I told them I couldn't stay any longer, I had to be on my way again, I was going to Warsaw. "Please stay," said Mrs. Topolewicz. "You have to help me. Władek is off to war. He was called up. He went to the town yesterday, they gave him a slip of paper . . ."

Mr. Topolewicz got up from the table. "It's true, I'm on my way today. But I'm afraid that by the time I reach my destination, the war will be over."

Suddenly my terror of the big man melted away. I went up to him and said loudly, "I want you to come back soon!"

It was sad without Mr. Topolewicz. The dogs would often run to the gate and wait for their master there. And at night they slept there. I waited with them.

On April 7, Michael came. When the dogs barked, I looked out the window and recognized him, although he had changed. I had been waiting for someone close, not Michael. One night, when I couldn't sleep, I had pictured a meeting with Aaron the rabbi's son, who was to be my husband. Aaron was sitting at the little table by the window, where Mrs. Topolewicz sat in the evenings and wrote down things in a fat notebook. Aaron smiled at me, but his mouth was red as if painted; he had black staring eyes and curly *peyis*. On the table lay a black prayer book, the one I found in the forest wrapped in a moldering tallis. I went up to Aaron, my future husband, and took the yarmulke from his head and stroked his curly hair.

About Michael I thought only once. It was when Busch, the German, stood over me in the dark barn, and I lay in the hay and stared at his small blue eyes and his quivering red mustache. "Don't be afraid," he said. "I'll help you. Just be very quiet, because German military police are in the house." I lay terrified, and remembered how we used to steal pears from Busch's orchard. Michael would give me a boost and then climb up after me. Huddled close together in the tree, we picked the juicy pears. I kept this scene, this memory in my mind in order not to cry out when Busch stood over me, and then later, when he left, closing the barn door behind him.

In the tree, Michael had his arm around me, and there too I trembled, but it was a different trembling. Michael's hand went to my neck, then there was a tug, and two little buttons went flying off my blouse, bouncing from branch to branch like pieces of hail. Michael kissed me on the cheek, the pear fell out of my hand, and I laughed. He said, "Sorry, Mirele," and that seemed even funnier. I picked another pear. "Bite!" I commanded. He took a bite. "My turn now!" I said and bit into the same pear in the same place. And so the two of us ate the juicy fruit in the tree of Busch the German.

Aaron would not return. He lay in a roadside ditch, his eyes open, his mouth open. He must have been screaming, and with that scream went to God. He left me to be the widow of a rabbi's son. A widow with a child who was never born, a child with curly hair like his father's, a chubby cherub of a baby boy who would have sucked at my breast, and I would have shown him proudly to Chanusia and Itka. But better not—my baby would have been crushed by the rifle butts of the Nazis.

Now, from the orchard of Busch the German, Michael had returned, and I was glad. He came into the house, and with him my whole town returned to me. He was my father, my mother, my grandma and grandpa, and the boy who once kissed me on the cheek. I sat down next to him, and Mrs. Topolewicz gave me the look that mothers give when they wish their daughters to be happy with their future husbands. Józia's white dog licked my hand. There were no tears or shouts of greeting, only quiet conversation, long silences, a few questions, a few answers, until finally only Michael spoke, and I listened intently.

Jacob

Little Jacob was a problem. He couldn't sleep in his bed. He would talk to himself, get up, and lie down again. He never cried or complained. Then they realized that he was hungry at night. After that, they gave him an extra two pieces of bread and a mug of grain coffee with milk before bedtime.

Józia began to teach him. They read a primer together; she made him recite the multiplication table; she brought in herbs, flowers, leaves of trees, telling him where each grew, giving the Polish and Latin names. "These are maple leaves," she might say, "and the Latin for the maple is *Acer platanoides*. This is milkweed, *Senchus arvensis*. This is the poppy, *Papaver nudicaule* . . ." Jacob nodded and promised to memorize everything, which made Józia happy and proud. "You got an A in Nature," she told him gravely, entering the grade in a notebook.

During supper I asked Józia where she learned the Latin names of the flowers and trees. "The lady from Warsaw taught me," she replied. "Mrs. Topolewicz used to be a teacher, though no one knew that. I was a good student. Jacob couldn't go to school, of course. Mama didn't know what Mrs. Topolewicz was doing, she found out only later, because it was a secret from the Germans. Mrs. Topolewicz keeps two black dogs on the property, because she is still afraid. She bought Bass and Tenor in Wólka Zagrodzka. A black dog is hard to see at night and difficult to shoot. The Germans shot at dogs."

"But your dog is white," I said.

"Atlas is a present of the first day after the War," Józia explained. "The forest gave him to me. I found him, he had a broken hind leg, but it mended in a month. Atlas is a postwar dog."

On Sunday, when Mrs. Topolewicz and Józia left for church, I padlocked the front door, left Atlas in the yard, took Jacob by the hand, and went to Mirele with him.

"Good morning," I said. "I brought a guest. This is Jacob Dawidowicz. Do you remember him?"

"I knew Dvoira Dawidowicz and David Dawidowicz, and I saw them in the marching column. They walked slowly, because Dawidowicz had a sack over his shoulder, and Mrs. Dawidowicz's legs were swollen and she walked with a cane."

"Mirele!" I said.

"What?"

"We can't stay here." I moved closer to her. Jacob sat by the window, silent. "We are three—that's all that's left of us. We can't stay here. The people here are good, but . . ."

"But?"

"One should earn a living. We have no money."

"True," she said.

"The little I brought back with me is used up."

"And I had good boots, but Mrs. Topolewicz traded them for flour, salt pork, and kasha."

"Also, we ought to find out if anyone else has survived," I added.

"I'm staying," Jacob said suddenly, breaking his silence. "I'll feed the crows—bits of bread. Someone has to. They flew over and saw our parents. . . ."

"You're coming with us," I said.

Jacob didn't answer. He sat motionless and looked out the window.

Mirele took me into another room, where there were two beds, a table, a chest of drawers, and two stools. On the wall hung a large picture of the Holy Virgin. "This is their bedroom," she said. "But Mr. Topolewicz is now in the army, so I sleep here with Mrs. Topolewicz. . . . She's in church, praying for him and for us. But where can you and I pray?" From under the bed she pulled out a little suitcase, opened it, took out a thick book bound in black, and held it in her hands. "I found this not far from here, on a forest path. It was wrapped in a tallis." She gave it to me.

I put it down on the table without opening it. "I can't pray. Praying didn't help us," I said.

She sat on the bed. "And I can't sleep. I'm always tired."

For me the best thing was not being hungry anymore. I ate my fill. Our soldiers brought sugar to the camp, and jam and bread and cake and soup and meat and potatoes. And we ate. My dream came true: I had enough to eat. And I stopped being afraid. We even got a little revenge. A few of us broke into a guard's apartment and smashed china, flowery teapots, dainty pink teacups, plates, saucers, crystal vases, ashtrays, sugar bowls, and we knocked all the glass out of the sideboards and ripped open feather pillows. The white fluff sank like snow, and the room turned lovely and white, reminding me of winter in our little town.

Winter meant silence, snow covering the roofs, the streets white and still. Quietly I made my way down those little white streets. Sometimes there was a cracking sound from a fence, and the snow squeaked under your boots. From the chimneys long light-gray columns of smoke rose straight into the sky. In the windows you could see candles burning or kerosene lamps. My family had a beautiful lamp with a large milk-glass shade. Lighting it was a major undertaking. You had to pour in kerosene, but not too much, or it would spill, and the wick had to be cleaned very carefully, and the glass dried. When the wick was lit, you had to watch to see that it burned evenly, without sooting. Then you fitted in the glass chimney and slowly turned the little wheel that regulated the length of the wick and therefore the flame, and that required the utmost accuracy. . . . It was my job to buy the kerosene. I bought it at Mr. Feierman's, who smelt of kerosene and floor wax even in the synagogue.

"Do you remember Mr. Feierman?" I asked Mirele.

"Yes," she said, sitting on the bed. "Here, sit next to me."

I sat beside her. "His son, Abraham, was handsome. When

he turned twenty-one, they took him into the army. Remember?"

"Of course I remember."

"And when he came home on leave, everybody admired him, the tall, smart lad in top boots and spurs, in the uhlan uniform. A week later he was back again, but not alone. With a lieutenant, this time. The townspeople looked out of their windows to see the two uhlans striding by in full battle gear. The lieutenant had come on a hunting visit to the squire of a nearby estate, and took along uhlan Feierman, and everything would have been fine if it hadn't been for Mr. Feierman.

"The old man decided to invite the lieutenant to his house for a Jewish meal. And so one day there was the lieutenant at the table, in the seat of honor, and opposite him sat a modest nineteen-year-old girl with beautiful black eyes in a pale face, Esther, Mr. Feierman's daughter. Naturally, the lieutenant was smitten. He got up, clicked his heels, went up to Esther, and kissed her hand. Then he left and fifteen minutes later returned with a bouquet of wildflowers picked by his own hand in the meadow behind the house. And he knelt and presented the flowers to her.

"Esther Feierman's wedding to Aaron Ryskin was to take place three weeks from then, but it didn't. One rainy night Esther disappeared. Abraham did not return, and the lieutenant stopped coming to our squire to hunt. Mr. Feierman continued to run his kerosene and floor wax business, but Mrs. Feierman fell sick and died just before the War. What happened after that, I don't know."

Mirele gave a sigh. "Poor Aaron Ryskin. He loved her so much."

"How do you know?"

"I saw the look in his eyes. . . . It was on the first day of the War. 'What's new with you, Aaron?' I asked. He didn't want to talk. Then I said that Esther was no good, a worthless woman. He told me that I didn't understand anything, that I was a fool and so were all the Jews in the shtetl. Esther, he said, was innocent. That pup of an officer had abducted her, and she might not even be alive. He said he was going to Warsaw to see a certain general and report this crime to him. But then the War . . ."

"I know what happened to Abraham," said Jacob, appearing in the doorway.

"Come in," I said, "and sit with us."

Jacob entered, but did not sit.

"You heard us?" Mirele asked.

"I have very good hearing. It's because I spent so much time in the dark. I heard the field mice talking, and the gnats and beetles. I heard the frogs in the swamp. And I heard Abraham Feierman. He was here, at the gamekeeper's. He came at night with Mr. Liwiec. They buried something behind the house. Abraham was called 'Silent.' That was his code name. And Mr. Liwiec was 'Fleet.' Now it is all right to talk about it."

"How do you know that it was Abraham?" I asked.

"From Józia." And he turned his back and went out.

Mirele finally said to me, "Jacob isn't going with us. Did you hear him? He has a mother. Mrs. Liwiec is his mother now. He has found somebody who loves him. After the killing and hatred there is still love. . . ."

I didn't believe in the love, but I told her silently that I would stay with her forever, that I needed her badly. Her hand, which I took into both of mine, was warm. I whispered, "Mirele . . ."

"I am Eve and you are Adam," she said in a flat voice. "But there is no Eden for us."

I nodded and put my arms around her and held her.

A Phone Call from London

"Hello! Mr. Tsigelstein?"

"Yes . . . ?"

"Benny?"

"No."

"Tsigelstein?"

"No."

"Is this Warsaw?"

"Yes."

"One yes, anyway. So is this Benny Tsigelstein?"

"I told you, no."

"I'm sorry."

"Just a minute . . . I know Tsigelstein."

"Look, I'm calling from London and it's costing me plenty. I have a number here for Benny Tsigelstein."

"It's the wrong one."

"What do you mean, the wrong Tsigelstein? There's another Tsigelstein?"

"That I don't know."

"But you said—"

"I meant, the wrong number."

"Ah! His number has changed. So would you give me, please, his new number?"

"I don't know it."

"Tell him that Mandelgold called from London, and that he should call me back, because for me it costs an arm and a leg, but for you in Poland the rates are cheaper."

"This is true, but how am I supposed to give Benny your message?"

"Any way you like."

"Hm."

"Can you hear me?"

"I hear you fine, but I don't know where Benny is."

"So wait till he gets home. And give him my number."

"I can't."

"What do you mean, you can't?"

"I haven't seen Benny Tsigelstein since September of nineteen thirty-nine."

"What?! Look, Mr. . . ."

"Rodziwił."

"What? Radziwiłł? Like the count?"

"Rodziwił. R as in Roman, O as in Olga, D as in David . . ."

"Enough, stop, I have to pay for this! What do you mean, Mr. Rodziwił, you haven't seen Benny since September of nineteen thirty-nine?"

"Just what I said. In fact, it's only from you, Mr. Mandelbrot, that I learned that Benny is alive."

"Mandelgold, not Mandelbrot! Moniek Man-del-gold! Benny is my cousin. His mother and my mother were sisters."

"In that case, I must know you!"

"From where? From London?"

"Now I remember you! You used to come over to Benny's. Skinny, red hair, freckles . . ."

"That was my brother, Nachum. I was tall, light-brown hair, no freckles."

"Moniek! We know each other after all! Don't tell me you don't remember Henny Rodziwił. I used to play poker with you, and you always cheated!"

"You're the one who lost his money and cried like a little girl?"

"That was me!"

"Oh, Lord, this is costing a fortune!"

"Good! That's how you'll pay back the money you took from me. After all these years . . . I always said I would get even with you!"

"All right . . . And how are you? What are you doing?"

"I got married, and we have a little daughter."

"And I got married and have a little son. And Benny?"

"I haven't seen—"

"I know, you already said. Here, write down my number: eight, zero, zero, eight, two, seven, one, four."

"I have it."

"Give me a call sometime!"

"I remember . . . Your whole family was redheaded. . . ."

"Yes, and that's why we survived. Everybody used to laugh at Dad, may he live a hundred years, but then the Germans didn't believe that a Jew could have red hair, freckles, and blue eyes."

"Your father's alive?"

"Dad was a gardener in a convent. . . . The nuns wanted to baptize him, but he got by without that. . . . I took him to London, and now he grows flowers in our garden."

"Give him my best!"

"Thanks. Well then, good-bye. . . . And tell Benny to call me!"

"Right!" Henry hung up and sat on the couch.

Mirka said, "I heard you. What a surprise! Was it a relative?"

"No, no . . . After all these years an old friend suddenly calls from London. . . . Oh my God, he didn't give me Benny's number! Now what'll I do?"

"Call him in London."

"Well, yes, I did write down his number. . . . But maybe Benny's in the phone book. Let me see . . . Tsa . . . Tse . . . Tsi . . . No. He's not here. I'll call information. Hello, information? The number, please, for Benny Tsigelstein. That is, Benon, or possibly Bruno Tsigelstein. Yes, Tsigelstein."

"Address, please."

"I don't have an address."

"Please hold . . . I'm sorry, but he's not listed."

"Thank you. Mirka, I'll kill myself! Information doesn't have a Tsigelstein."

"Then call London." She smiled.

"London, all right, I'm dialing . . . Hello? Moniek? What? Damn, the connection's bad, I can't hear!"

"Is that you again, Henny?"

"It's me. . . . Listen, you didn't give me Benny's number!"

"I didn't? Hold on."

"I don't want to hold on. This is costing money."

"It's not that expensive at your end. Here we are. But listen . . . Have you seen Dvoira Katzberg? You know, from Nowolipki. . . . And what about Shimon Gotberg?"

"Come on, give me Benny's number, Moniek, don't play games. You earn your money in pounds sterling, but mine comes in zlotys, and zlotys don't go far."

"Just a minute, Dad wants to talk to you!"

"Henny! It's me, old Mandelgold! How is your mama?"

"She died in the Ghetto."

"Ah. And your papa?"

"And my brother."

"Terrible, terrible, they didn't have red hair. . . . It was hell, yes. And me, I grow flowers these days, and my hair is all white now."

"Mr. Mandelgold, do you know Benny Tsigelstein's phone number? It's important . . ."

"No, I don't, Henny, but you I remember well. I used to wipe your little nose, it was always full of snot. Ran like a faucet . . . Hay fever. Sister Eugenia had hay fever, too."

"Your sister?"

"No, in the convent."

"Mr. Mandelgold, about Benny's number . . ."

"Moniek says you should call him in an hour."

"No, let him call me."

Henry hung up and sighed.

"Well?" Mirka asked.

"I always had trouble with him. The whole family was absentminded. His mother, father, and brother. How did they get through the War?"

"Maybe by not paying attention."

"Impossible."

"There's the phone ringing again, answer it."

"Hello!"

"Is this Warsaw?"

"Yes."

"Henny?"

"Yes?"

"Five, four, six, six, seven, one. That's Benny's number. Good-bye."

"Hello? Hello? How do you like that? He hung up on me. What a skinflint! But wait a minute. . . . Mirka, how come Moniek said, before, that he misdialed, when Benny's number isn't even close to ours?"

"That's peculiar," Mirka said.

"Well, I'll try the number now. . . . Hello!"

"Yes? This is Dr. Kierowski's residence."

"Oh . . . Could I speak to your husband?"

"My father."

"I'm sorry, I thought I was talking to Mrs. . . ."

"Mama died."

"Forgive me."

"Papa's here. Hold on."

"Yes?"

"Benny!"

"Excuse me?"

"Tsigelstein?"

"You must have the wrong number."

"This is Henry Rodziwił speaking. My number is five, one, one, seven, zero, two, nine. I have greetings for you from London, from—"

"There's no such person here."

"I'm sorry. Good-bye."

"Well, what now?" Mirka asked.

"I don't know. . . . It may be he or it may not be."

"I'm going to get us some lunch. But you sit here a while, maybe someone will call now from New Zealand or Japan. There! It's ringing . . ."

"Hello? Rodziwił here."

"You called me a moment ago. . . ."

"Yes?"

"I have a request. Cross out my phone number and forget it, forever. And tell that to the person in London. Just forget it."

"I'm terribly sorry, I didn't mean to . . ."

"I understand."

"But you have my number."

"I'll throw it out."

"You don't have to do that. But I'll convey your message to the party in London. And I really am sorry."

"Good-bye, then."

Mirka returned from the kitchen.

"Well, what did he say?"

"That wasn't Benny Tsigelstein. Benny left Warsaw."

"Where to?"

"Destination unknown."

They sipped their tea in silence.

Syndrome

When Leon returned to Warsaw after the War, he couldn't find his house. All day he wandered among the ruins, and in the evening he met a girl. Together they crossed the rubble of the Ghetto to the Old City. In the cellar of a ruined house she had a bed, a chest, three chairs, and a shelf with two plates, a glass, and a mug.

"If this suits you, you can stay," said Julka. He stayed.

One morning he woke up and saw that the shelf had only one plate, and the mug was gone. She did not return that day or the next. That was when he started drinking. In the summer of 1947, in Grzybowski Square, not far from the Church of All Saints, where Twarda Street used to run, he met Aaron. They sat down on a low wall and talked, then took a little path through some ruins. Aaron led him to a building, the only synagogue left in Warsaw.

"So something did survive," said Leon.

"What about us?" asked Aaron.

"What about us? What do I do with myself now? I copy

numbers, compute costs of building, rebuilding, the repair of one apartment house, of another . . . My desk is by a window, but I am always hot. And when I go out to a construction site, I am too cold. . . ."

"You could make something of yourself. You were the best student in your high school class," Aaron said.

"Maybe," Leon said. "But I don't want to, I can't."

Aaron gave him his address. "Come over, have a talk with my mother and father," he urged. "Maybe together we'll figure something out."

"All right, I'll come," Leon promised.

But he envied Aaron for having a mother and a father, so he didn't go. In the evenings he wandered through the town. Often he crossed the bridge and found himself in a different Warsaw. He would step into a bar or a restaurant, talk with chance acquaintances, drink vodka or beer with them. Sometimes he treated them, at other times they treated him. One morning he woke up in Jadwiga's bed.

"I brought you here," she said, "because at the bar you mentioned Smocza Street and Nowolipie, and Karmelicka Street, and that was my territory before the War. I had a good clientele. They all died in the Ghetto, you survived. You're the first customer from my own district."

"I'm not a customer." He tried to get out of bed, but Jadwiga put her arms around him and kissed him on the lips. "I'm sorry, I didn't mean that. I love you."

"So fast?"

"No, not that fast. I've seen you a dozen times. You drink."

"And you?" he asked, sitting up in the bed.

"I am afraid," she said. "I am afraid of getting sick. I don't really like to drink, but I have to, in my profession. During the Occupation I had a rest, though." She laughed. "I didn't drink or go to bed with boys and grandpas."

"Did you feel better?"

"Yes. Pure as a virgin." She jumped out of the bed, ran to the sideboard, and pulled out a bottle. "You see? Here is booze, and today I pour it down the drain." And she emptied the bottle into the sink. "Now we'll have a chaste glass of tea with saccharine."

After breakfast she lit a cigarette and announced: "Say the word, love, and I stop working."

"I don't believe you," he said. "I don't believe anybody."

He didn't move in with Jadwiga, but took a room nearby, on Ząbkowska Street at Grzesiek's, an old and deaf World War I veteran. Jadwiga visited him often.

"I took time off," she said. "My project today is your apartment."

She tidied up, took his wash to lame Janka to be laundered, did his shopping, bought him a shirt and long underwear.

"Listen, Leon," she would say, "let's go abroad. They don't know me there. We can get married. I'll even convert to Judaism. The God is the same, the sins are the same, what do I stand to lose?"

Leon smiled. "There are three obstacles. The first: the graves of my parents, grandparents, aunts, uncles, and brothers are here. The second: my character. The third: your character."

On Sunday, waking up late in the morning, he saw Jadwiga in his room. She was sitting at the table and writing.

"What are you writing?" he asked, surprised that she could write.

"That I'm leaving, that I've had enough of you, that I'll do harm to myself, what harm, I don't know yet. . . ."

"Does everybody have to leave?" was wrenched from him, but he said no more.

"I could stay, but . . ."

"Go, I'm not holding you back! I knew it would end this way."

She got up from the table and came closer. "Remember, shithead, you come from my old territory, and you can't change that! Ever!" And she tore up the unfinished letter and left.

In the bars it was said that she left Warsaw, or else that she was in jail. Someone claimed that a friend of his had seen her in the country and that she had married a wealthy farmer.

On New Year's Eve, 1951, Leon had a special table set for him in the bar. He sent the band a hundred-zloty note. "Let's have a march," he called to them. "I like marches!" He lowered his head, holding an empty glass in his hand, his eyes half closed.

He was a child riding a hobbyhorse, playing soldier, waving a stick in his small hand. But it wasn't a stick, it was a saber. He slashed with it, left, right . . . He dismounted and ran about the park, an Indian chief, an Iroquois. He got up on a bench. They were all shouting: "Long live Great Bear, who conquered Red Mustang!" Then the Indians galloped to the river, he in front, the fastest. Suddenly someone took him by the hand. His mother! Yes, there was once a mother, there was once a father, and brothers . . . But what was this, the music had stopped!

"Play on, I am paying . . . play a czardas!"

Violins. It got to him, the way the violins sobbed. The violinist in front raised his instrument higher, the bow moved faster on the strings, until it disappeared, and the fingers on the strings disappeared, and the violin disappeared, and the violinist. Only his sad eyes remained.

Large, dark eyes. *She* had eyes like that. And took them to the gas chamber with her. To the oven. He didn't see her body shriveled in the fire, he smelled it. All the bodies . . . That smell stayed with him. The bodies were carted there in special barrows, and turned to ashes. He had bought himself off at the *Umschlagsplatz,* the marshaling yard, with a gold watch and a ring, but she was taken away. After that, there was no sense in buying oneself off, but they pushed him into the railway car . . .

"Hey, bandmaster, music!" He was better now. The oven, Helena was gone, the ashes were gone. There was no point in crying. Why, so others could see and point at him?

He turned around, signaled the waiter. "Franek! Another bottle, and tell them to play something more cheerful." The next thing he knew, there was a hunchbacked man sitting opposite him.

"May I?" said the man. "All the other seats are taken."

"Be my guest," said Leon, and poured wine into the hunchback's empty glass.

The man took a sip and said: "I have a hump, sir, and yet you drink with me like a comrade. Waiter! A carafe, please, and two steaks tartare with eggs! So . . . so I wash my hump down with vodka, as if to dissolve it in alcohol. Ha, ha! See, the hump is gone! It's gone because I'm drinking now. When

I stop, it comes back. Excuse my asking, but have you ever been ashamed of yourself, I mean, of what you are? A silly question, you are a handsome man. . . . But I am constantly ashamed, except when I drink. When I drink, I'm a different person. No one thinks that a hunchback man can love a normal woman. But at home I have a collection of photographs. Famous women, beauties, stars of stage and screen, I cut them out of magazines, and not one of them is a hunchback. I drink to your health, sir. Ah, but now they are playing a czardas. That violin gets under a man's skin, it makes one weep. Are you by any chance related to Michael Nussenbaum? You look just like him."

"There's no Michael Nussenbaum in my family," said Leon.

"A pity! The Nussenbaums lived with me during the Occupation."

"You saved people during the Occupation?" Leon asked, incredulous.

"Ah! You say 'save.' I don't call that saving, I call that looking out for my kind. After all, they were hunchbacks. . . . Not physically, of course, but they were people like me. Afflicted. Yes, that's right, the Nussenbaums with their daughter, little Rosie, and her baby brother. We dug a tunnel under the privy, and that's where they survived the Occupation. Practically in shit, sir, practically in shit. Imagine what they endured. I'll take you to see it, to see where people lived then to stay alive. . . . But I let my tongue run away with me. Waiter! The check, please."

"No," said Leon, putting some bills on the table. "You are my guest."

The band played a waltz, and the hunchback disappeared. Leon, reeling a little, made it to the checkroom, but was told that the hunchback had left.

"Another one gone . . ." Leon said to the attendant. "Always somebody leaving."

That autumn, Leon fell from the scaffolding. Checking on a construction cost estimate, he slipped on a wet plank on the second floor. It was not a bad fall, but after that he stopped drinking.

"This is your last warning," Dr. Putrak said. "Tomorrow will be too late."

Two years later, Leon ran into Jadwiga.

"What are you up to these days?" she asked him.

"Looking for you," he said.

"Still drinking?"

"No—how about you?"

"I'm in town for only a few hours." And after a moment she added, "I've changed. I have a husband and children."

"See you, then," he said and turned away.

"Wait!" she called.

He ran, jumped on a streetcar, and rode to the end of the line. Then he walked until he found himself at the railroad station. He got on a train, but had to get off at the next station because he didn't have a ticket. He went to the ticket office to buy one, but the ticket office was closed. On a country road, he saw a little girl with a handful of wildflowers.

"Let me buy your flowers," he said to the girl.

"They aren't for sale," she answered. "Someone gave them to me."

This crushed Leon. He asked the girl if he could have a flower as a gift. She gave him three. He knelt down, returned two, and the third he put in her hair just over her forehead.

Next morning, he awoke in the ward for alcoholics. Getting out of the hospital, he went to Dr. Putrak. The doctor said he would have to change his job.

Leon made a decision. On Saturday he waited for Aaron outside the synagogue at Grzybowski Square. After two hours he met Boruch Blic, whom he had known before the War. Boruch lived by himself in the Grochów quarter; he took Leon home with him.

"I'm a shoemaker now," Boruch said. "I can't complain. I'll take you in on one condition. No drinking."

"Done," Leon agreed.

They worked together, and Leon learned fairly quickly how to resole boots and sew little straps on ladies' shoes. He came to like his work. Each pair of shoes said something about its owner. A badly worn pair meant poverty, he thought—but he soon realized that the poor took care of their footwear because they had to, so neglect meant something else.

This period, living with Boruch, was one of happiness in Leon's life. He got to know every customer and talked with them. The ladies smiled at him because he was good-looking, intelligent, and interesting. Mrs. Rozwilska declared outright that Leon ought to be in the movies. "You're a born leading man," she said. For the first time, surrounded by pumps and sandals, Leon began to think of the future.

One day, he picked up a high-heeled lady's pump of fine green leather with a strap and silver buckle. "Now this," he said to Boruch, "is beautiful."

"Yes," Boruch assented. "Good workmanship. Custom-made . . ."

"Whose is it?"

"I don't know," said Boruch, scratching his bald head. "It was brought by a middle-aged lady, but she wears a six, and this looks to me like a five."

The middle-aged lady came the next day. She picked up the mended green pumps and left. But Leon couldn't stop thinking about the woman who wore the green fives with the strap and silver buckle. Who was she? What did she look like? Was she young, old, tall, short, blonde, brunette, or perhaps a redhead like Helena or Jadwiga?

Boruch, returning from the synagogue, said to him, "You sit at home all the time. Go outside, take a walk."

Leon went for a walk. On Hetmanska Street he saw a woman wearing green shoes. He followed her at a distance, but she got into a taxi on the corner and was driven away. . . .

"Back already?" Boruch asked. "Why so soon?"

"I feel at home here," Leon said. "I'm afraid I might walk too far."

But one day he went out, rising very early, while Boruch was still asleep. The streetcars had only just started their rounds, the milk trucks were pulling up to closed shops, and the janitors were opening gates and scrubbing sidewalks. Grochowska Street was quiet and deserted. Leon went as far as Targowa Street and stopped at a closed bar. He stood there a while, then proceeded to Ząbkowska Street, where he knocked at a door on the second floor. A sleepy girl opened it.

"Who are you looking for?"

"The deaf man."

"He's dead."

"You mean in prison?"

"Yes. And you? Did you just get out?"

He turned away. The girl closed the door, leaving him alone on the landing.

At noon Leon went to the synagogue in Grzybowski Square, but it was closed. He sat down on the steps of the Catholic church and watched the women who were working on the lawn. One raked, another collected dry leaves and paper and put them in a trash bin, a third weeded. Wanting to help them, he got up from his seat, but found he was too tired.

There was a new doctor, not Dr. Putrak: young, tall, with a shock of black hair and a half-fledged mustache and beard. He was calm, matter-of-fact, and pleasant.

"You're young," said Leon.

"Yes, it shows." The doctor smiled. "I've been here only a few weeks."

This made Leon smile too, but he hid the smile with his hand. After a pause he said, "Doctor, I don't want to answer a lot of questions."

"I had hoped we could have a talk, informally," said the doctor.

"That's different," said Leon. "They"—he pointed backward with his thumb—"interrogate, one question after another, in their white coats. Take off that doctor's coat, and we can talk."

The doctor took off his coat and hung it over a chair.

"Yesterday, I read about a kind of sickness you people call 'concentration-camp syndrome.' One could just as well talk about a post-ghetto syndrome. . . . I suffer from both. And would like to be cured of them. . . . I stand at windows watching the free come and go." Leon got up and went to the window, opened it, then quickly closed it again and returned to his chair. "Yesterday I told the psychologist lady that I sleep at night. I told her all kinds of lies. . . .

"Horace says it's sweet and honorable to die for one's country. They taught us that in high school. . . . I'm a shoemaker, but I know Latin. I nail down heels and recite *Dulce et decorum est pro patria mori.* In the camp, plenty of dying for the fatherland went on, but none of us wore a uniform or the four-cornered cap with the eagle on it. We died in convict stripes or naked—in jails, in yards, in police cells. It depended. . . . And I'm alive because I was lucky. I came to nobody's attention. Why? The question torments me. Could someone have protected me, given his life so that I would not be noticed? Someone I don't know and never saw? Or there might have been several of them. . . .

"In the bar they yelled at me to stop talking about the camp. They told me to shut up. At the office, too. So I stopped. Sometimes I think that it was easier to live through the camp than it is to live through the memories of it.

"Kulas, the Kapo, wept at the ramp as he herded Jewish girls from the freight car to the gas chambers, but an instant later he clubbed a cripple who had hidden under the car, then forced him into a truck filled with screaming people. The truck started up, a child fell from it. Kulas held the child in his arms and whispered, 'I would hide him, but where?' 'There's no place,' I said. 'You know that!' The truck was far away by this time. 'Put the kid on the next truck!' roared

Kulas, handing me the terrified child. 'He is going to the gas, is that clear?'

"'I bought shoes from Misha, a Ukrainian. I paid a high price: bread, my worn slippers, some string, and cigarettes. Kulas screamed: 'You bastard! Trying to be high society, eh? Take those shoes off before I get angry!' I took them off, he put them on. 'Tight at the toes, lucky for you.'

"'I ate apple peels, bread crusts, rutabaga. Now, cake revolts me. I think of the crusts. Of the sugar beets, the nettle soup, the boiled potatoes sweet from being frozen.

"'What is hunger? Hunger is a beast that lives in your belly, in your chest, in your head. . . . It gnaws at you, squeezes you. First you feel an ache, then weakness, then a greater ache. The beast makes you do things, you are its slave. We bartered. Soup for tobacco, tobacco for bread, bread for apples, apples for lard, lard for bread. Around and around, back and forth, our marketplace.

"'Kazik was from Warsaw. At first he was afraid. Then Boltz took a fancy to him. 'You are like a girl,' Boltz would say and pat his cheeks. Kazik gave Boltz smiles. A week later, Boltz was transferred. 'Who will I smile at now?' Kazik asked. I told him: 'You can't smile at these cavemen.' 'I want to live!' he said. I told him: 'Play up to one of them, and it'll be all right. Play up to the next, and he'll blow your head off. You can't tell with them.' Kazik was shot dead by a guard they called Pagliacci.

"'The stripes we wore, the zebra rags. Now, whenever I see stripes, I smell the reek of laborers, slaves, and hear the Kapo's voice: 'Attention, transport approaching!' And nobody believes me, none of you know what the smell is like, or the taste of rutabaga, a raw sugar beet, a piece of bread picked out of the mud in the road.

"I run into Kazik here. I know he's dead, I know that Pagliacci shot him, but I still run into him. He'll be walking, looking into store windows. He'll get into a streetcar, and when someone jostles him, he'll say: 'I beg your pardon, I was killed at eleven thirty-five in nineteen forty-three by the guard Pagliacci.' 'Go to hell!' the passengers shout. 'Stop blocking the aisle! Move!' Or I'll see, on the other side of the street, in the crowd, someone I know from the camp. The figure vanishes, I can't catch up with it, so I go back home and wait. I have lunch, I read the paper or a book, but really I am waiting. I am waiting, and nobody comes. It's hell, this waiting. . . ."

"Others were in camps too, weren't they?" the doctor said.

"Yes, but they say nothing, they're afraid to talk. They talked after their return, but then they stopped."

Leon fell silent. He searched the doctor's face, then lowered his head and said: "My drinking started after the War. When I got back to Warsaw, I couldn't find my house. . . ."

"I think I can help," said the young doctor.

"By all means, help me," said Leon, again going over to the window. "If you find Julka or Jadwiga or the hunchback, or the girl with the wildflowers, I'll stop drinking." He turned and faced the doctor. "But you don't believe me. I can see you don't believe me. . . ."

"Well, we may not be able to find the girl with the wildflowers," said the doctor, smiling.

Leon jumped up on the window ledge, leaned over, bent his knees, kicked, and was gone from sight.

"Leon!" cried the doctor.

"Don't worry, I'm not hurt! It's not that high! I'll be seeing you, Doctor!"

"Leon! Leon!" called the doctor, but Leon ran into the busy street and disappeared around a corner.

On the Corner

Walking down the street: hunchback Haskiel and blind Abram. Haskiel comes from a little town, but Abram was born in Warsaw and lived here until 1939. They met at Samarkand in 1942. They were standing in line for hot water, and that is how they got acquainted. Later, over tea, they talked about Poland. It made Abram late for work, so he had to give a reason to the foreman. He said: "I met a relative from the banks of the Vistula, and we talked and forgot the time."

Now Haskiel is leading Abram through the streets of Warsaw—the old Warsaw, because Abram recognizes no other.

"You say we're at the corner of Nowolipie and Smocza?" Abram asks.

"Yes. You asked that before. Word of honor, I'm telling the truth."

"And the streetcar tracks are here?"

"They are."

"They turn from Smocza into Nowolipie and from Nowolipie into Żelazna?"

"We haven't come to Żelazna yet."

"I know that. You don't have to give me lessons. I could show *you* the way." Abram is angry.

Haskiel tries to calm him. "What are you getting worked up about? Everything is fine!"

"I don't hear people, I don't hear the streetcar bells. I don't hear anything! What, have I gone deaf, too? I haven't had a look at the world since June, nineteen forty-four, because of these damned cataracts, but I've learned to hear the world. My hearing's good. . . ."

"You hear nothing, because nothing's happening."

"Don't play the teacher with me! How can nothing be happening? There are shops and houses here, aren't there? Shops, people passing. . . . On the corner is Mr. Sewek's barbershop, a newspaper stand, and over there a streetcar stop and a greengrocer, and in the gateway two women selling bagels, I know those women, they're real balabustehs. And right on the other side of the street is Mrs. Scheyndl. She sits beside her stand, not behind it, selling candy, lollipops, chocolate bars—Domański, Plutos, Fuchs bars. And if you turn just a little to the right, you'll see on the sidewalk a couple of two-wheeled carts knocked together out of thick planks, like small platforms with poles. Along the poles runs a length of coarse rope, which ends, as you can see, in something like a horse collar. The owner of each cart fits the collar on himself. . . . Here, for instance, is Josef Boim slipping the collar over his left shoulder, holding the pole with his left hand, and shouting: 'Hoyoh!' You ask what they haul?"

"I'm not asking."

"They haul anything. They charge less than Hartwig Movers, because while Hartwig Movers move using a flatcar on rubber tires drawn by a pair of bays, Josef Boim moves with one little cart, and even if it takes him two trips, he does it faster and better. A man hauls more neatly than a horse. Geldings are strong, yes, but also slow, lazy, stupid. . . . Take me across the street now, but be careful. Ah, I finally hear some voices. . . . It must be those two Jews discussing politics. I should explain. . . . The first, the one with the little reddish beard, is Mendel Haint, the other, the one without a beard, is Moses Puch. Amusing names, no? Haint, like the name of the Warsaw newspaper. And Puch means down, feathers, but he doesn't sell quilts, he is the owner of a little herring shop, and Mr. Haint has his soap business right next door. Whenever I passed the herring shop and the soap shop, I'd see Mr. Haint in his doorway and Mr. Puch in his doorway, no matter what time of day, and they'd be debating world politics. They predicted wars, coups, resignations of premiers and cabinet ministers, economic crises, and upheavals on every continent. Now, there was something to listen to! Mr. Haint was the expert on European affairs, and Mr. Puch specialized in South America. Sometimes they'd be joined by Mr. Bodo, a dealer in neckties and plaster of Paris—no relation to the movie actor Eugeniusz Bodo. This necktie man's first name was Schloime. He carried his merchandise in a little green suitcase. The plaster he sold at the market between Leszno Street and Nowolipie, the ties on Muranowska and Gęsia streets, up to Przebieg Street, past the parade grounds. . . . Are you listening?"

"I'm listening."

"Let's stop here for a while and rest." Abram lifts his head, his lips move, he smiles and says something to himself.

Haskiel, meanwhile, studies the street, seeing it as it really is: wide, bright, with the houses freshly stuccoed. There are no streetcar stops, no stand where Mrs. Scheyndl sells lollipops and chocolate bars, no carts or porters. He doesn't hear or see Mr. Haint, Mr. Puch, or Mr. Bodo. People in warm overcoats, lined jackets, and sheepskin vests hurry past; some teenagers make a dash for a bus; a young woman pushes a child in a baby carriage, avoiding a mud puddle on the sidewalk. Now a little Syrena sedan pulls up, a man with a ginger goatee gets out, and Haskiel is struck by the idea that this might be a son of Mr. Haint or even Mr. Haint himself, so he asks:

"Tell me, Abram, did Mr. Haint have a son?"

"No, he has four daughters, to his misfortune."

"Why to his misfortune?"

"Because he has to come up with a dowry for each of them," explains Abram. "Mr. Puch, now, has three sons, and Mr. Bodo is an old bachelor. The arithmetic of this is that the three Puch sons plus Mr. Bodo could marry the four Misses Haint, but between you and me, they could do better."

Haskiel lets his eyes wander over the street again. It's covered with snow, but one can make out four parallel streetcar rails sunk into the asphalt and describing an arc from Smocza to Nowolipie, where they all end as if cut off with a knife.

"You could get married," says Abram, "you are younger than me. There are still some Jewish women. . . . You could find one."

Haskiel says nothing. He can't tell Abram, who is a pious Jew, that he is going with Alicja. He doesn't know himself what will come of this acquaintance.

Alicja is a widow. She lives in a room on the third floor of an old tenement posted for demolition. Each time Haskiel climbs the wooden stairs, he wonders when the creaking rotten planks will collapse under him and take him plunging into the cellar. Alicja laughs at his fear: "I am bigger than you and I am not afraid, but you, my little grasshopper, are all atremble." He likes it when she hugs him to her mighty breasts and calls him her little grasshopper. Sometimes she calls him Tailor Straightpin, Tailor Buttonhole, or Haskiel the Bobbin. Alicja is a seamstress who works at home, sewing men's trousers for the tailor Mr. Eugeniusz Lubirski, whose shop has an elegant Warsaw clientele, including even foreigners. Haskiel helps her, sewing on buttons or zippers, ripping out basted seams, or cleaning the old Singer machine, which Alicja found in the rubble of the Ghetto in 1945. Alicja's apartment smells of fresh bread, but the smell isn't from baking, it's from the dry rolls she cuts into slices to make zwieback on the stove. There's always a paper bag full of zwieback ready in her sideboard, just in case.

"What's on your mind, Haskiel?" Abram asks, noticing his companion's long silence.

"I was just thinking," Haskiel answers, "that all around us are people who have apartments, wives, children, a kitchen, a stove, a wardrobe . . ."

Saying this, Haskiel is reminded of yesterday's conversation with Alicja. He was sewing a button onto a pair of gray pin-striped trousers while she poured tea, when suddenly she turned and said: "My precious little hunchbacked Jew, you bring out the mother in me, I can't help it. You're a tailor, I'm a seamstress, together we'll manage all right. I may be a Protestant, and you of the Mosaic faith, but we'll be married by a clerk in the Registrar's Office, who's bound to be an atheist. After that, we'll write a request to the Housing Office, for a large, comfortable apartment. . . ."

"I know many people here," says Abram, interrupting Haskiel's train of thought. "At Number Sixty-five there"—Abram points—"in the basement lives the porter Feivel with his wife and five children, and higher up lives a kosher butcher, who has three rooms plus a kitchen, and a wife and a mother-in-law beside his parents, also a deaf aunt, but only one son, Adam."

"There's no Number Sixty-five here, the street ends at Thirty-one, and on the opposite side is Twenty-eight."

Abram, ignoring this, continues:

"Adam was a few years older than me, but we became friends. We went to the movies. Or we would go to the Jewish theater on Dzielna Street, or sometimes to boxing matches held at the Nowość Theater. Adam loved boxing, he was strong and agile. He told me once that he was going to run away to America and become the world boxing champion. And imagine, he really did run away, only it wasn't to America but to Kraków. Later he returned to Warsaw and became a famous motorcycle stunt man. He had an act called the Wall of Death, with a crazy Catholic woman from Kraków, Paulina."

Haskiel is interested. "What was it, this act?"

"The Wall of Death was a giant barrel open at the top, wide as half our yard, and almost as high as the second floor. . . . You entered the barrel by climbing up the outside on a little stairway. There were seats and standing room at the top, from where you had a view of the inside of the barrel. Inside, Adam performed. In a black bodysuit, black helmet, and black top boots, looking like the devil himself, he mounted a black motorcycle, started it by kicking some sort of pedal, turned something at the handlebar, and with a great roar started riding around and around the barrel, first slowly, then faster and faster, until after several minutes he was near the top. Then he blindfolded himself with a black cloth and kept spinning. In the second half of the act, Miss Paulina, a slim little blonde, mounted a second motorcycle, this one red. And she wore a red bodysuit, a red beret, and red top boots. She circled the barrel counterclockwise while Adam went clockwise. Around and around they buzzed like mad, missing each other by inches. Meanwhile, among the public, people fainted, kids squealed, and young men ogled the figure of blonde Paulina, who went by the title of Miss Motorcycle."

"I've seen a thing or two in my day," says Haskiel, "but that was one I missed."

"Now, on the third floor lived Hanka Goldweisel. She once invited me to her birthday party. It happened this way: Hanka's mother met my mother in Mr. Meisel's soda shop. While Mr. Meisel was filling our two syphons, Mrs. Goldweisel told my mother of the birthday and said: 'I'm inviting your son for cocoa on Saturday at five P.M. He should dress up. There will be youngsters there from good families.' When we got home, I rebelled. I said I wasn't going to the birthday party and that I hated youngsters from good families because they were stuck-up and mean. Their presents were sure to be better and more expensive. Father was on my side and produced a weighty argument: Mr. Goldweisel went to synagogue only on Yom Kippur, and on Pesach the Goldweisels ate *chometz.* Mother, more progressive, said that that didn't matter to her, because my future was at stake. With Hanka Goldweisel I would make a good match. . . . But Hanka went away, right before the War, to join her grandmother in England."

"And did you go to her birthday party?"

"Yes, and I drank cocoa, ate cream pastries, and played lotto with them."

"So your fiancée left for England?"

"She wasn't my fiancée. She was ten at the time."

"And you?"

"Eleven, almost."

"When I was eleven, I herded goats," Haskiel says. "Four goats. One was ours, one was my grandmother's, one belonged to my other grandmother, and the fourth was our neighbor's. All of them had blue eyes. . . . In Warsaw there are no goats."

"Here on Nowolipie, Number Sixty-six, in the second courtyard, is a cow shed with two cows in it, but I haven't seen a goat."

"My goats," Haskiel goes on, "were the spit and image of our neighbor Mr. Zalman. He was gray, had a gray little chin-beard, blue eyes, kept moving his lower jaw, so that when he took his cap off, one expected to see little goat horns. . . ."

"I'm not finished," Abram rebukes Haskiel. "On the fourth floor lives Isaac Ton. His father, Ephraim Ton, has a glazier's shop on Smocza Street. I remember once visiting the shop with Isaac. I never saw so much glass in one place in my life. Thick sheets, medium sheets, and very thin sheets. The place was full of sawdust, and the walls were covered with mirrors large and small, square and round, in frames of wood or metal, plain or fancy. . . . We looked at ourselves in those mirrors, and Isaac said the shop was full of Isaacs wherever he turned. There were plenty of me too, and in one huge mirror I saw myself distorted into a monkey. This was a special mirror, seven feet by ten, made to order for Mr. Kornshtein. Itzik Kornshtein lived on Nowolipie, somewhere near the cyclodrome. He was in the entertainment business. He rented empty shop fronts for short periods and put on a three-dimensional photography show called Photoplasticon, and had acts featuring various freaks of nature. The heaviest man in the world, for instance, or the smallest woman in Europe, or 'the human horse,' whose eyes were almost on the sides of his head. There were women with necks like giraffes and midgets who danced the waltz or tango on a table set with plates and a tureen of hot soup. Every time I went to one of those shows with Isaac, I got angry, afraid, hot and sweaty, and once I even peed in my pants."

"In our shtetl we didn't have freaks," says Haskiel, rubbing his frozen hands together. "Occasionally a magician came by in a top hat and tuxedo, with his wife, who was so beautiful that many of the men went to the show instead of *schul.* Just before the War, a trapeze artist from a circus passed through. He hung his trapeze from a limb of the tallest tree in town, near Mr. Zalman's house, and did his tricks there. All sorts of gymnastic things, dangerous. . . . The money was collected by his daughter, a little girl dressed in the folk costume of Kraków. . . . In Samarkand, twice I dreamt that I was hanging from that trapeze and couldn't get down."

"You have interesting dreams, Haskiel."

"Yes, more interesting than my life. I wish I could dream all the time. . . ."

Haskiel falls silent, and so the two of them stand there at

the edge of the sidewalk, right by a newspaper stand, and freezing people walk by, hurrying from their jobs to the warmth of their apartments. Haskiel is tempted to tell Abram, finally, that the things that Abram talks about, they all belong to the past, that there aren't any old tenements or Jews with sidelocks here, or narrow little shops crammed with mended sacks, boxes, and barrels of sauerkraut or pickled herring. That there are no more carts with poles or old women selling bagels. That he, Abram, is blind and dreaming.

But Haskiel says nothing, because when he turns, he sees that Abram is slowly tilting his head now to one side, now to the other, smiling, and one doesn't often see Abram smile.

A Strange Country

It was on this street, where I have my newsstand, that Dora lived. You reached the apartment of her parents by the first courtyard, but her window faced the second courtyard. Faced a wall, actually. Though the wall had two openings through which you could look into the courtyard of the next building.

I sell cigarettes, newspapers, matches, postcards, soap.

Mendel Bir was standing by the bench at the bus stop, holding a package wrapped in gray paper and tied with black string.

"What have you got there, Mr. Bir?" I asked.

He only smiled, then boarded the bus. Was it Mendel Bir or wasn't it? It looked like him, but it could have been his son or even his grandson.

But Chaya Sklepik I recognized by the kerchief on her head. The kerchief you could never tell the color of. I think it depended on the time of day, or whether it was sunny or cloudy. Sometimes it would be red, and sometimes, probably after laundering, a dark brick color. When the Ghetto walls were closed, the kerchief was the color of dirty sand. Just before the destruction of the Ghetto, it was like the ashes that had settled in the yard of our burnt-out tenement near Nowolipie.

Not long ago, I was walking down the street, returning from work, when suddenly out of a dark gateway stepped a man.

"Excuse me," he said, "can you tell me where Gęsia Street is now?"

"It used to be here," I answered the stranger. "But there hasn't been a Gęsia Street for some time."

"What, did they move it to another neighborhood?"

"You can't move a street." I took a look at the man: large dark eyes, bushy eyebrows, a hooked nose, a graying mustache. Something odd about him . . .

"And Lubecki Street," he continued, "where have they put it? I can't find either one. Before the War I lived at the intersection of Gęsia and Lubecki. Perhaps they still exist somewhere. . . ."

"No, that's impossible."

"Anything is possible, my dear man. Anything, even that I, Pincus Szczulewicz, should return from Haiti."

"You lived in Haiti?"

"You think that's strange? Well, not only do I come from Haiti but my wife is Chinese, and my daughter is married to a Pole. Janek has come here with me. He's from Kalisz. You can bump into Jews and Poles anywhere, even in the Congo or Tierra del Fuego."

“Why are you here?”

“A legitimate question. I'm looking for my twin brother. I heard he was alive.”

“He, too, has a mustache?”

“I don't understand.”

“If you both have a mustache, you'll recognize each other, but if he doesn't . . .”

“Then we won't?”

“What did you say your name was?”

“Szczulewicz, Pincus Szczulewicz, but in Haiti my name is different.”

“They have a ghetto there, too? You had to change your papers?”

“No, no . . . They couldn't pronounce Szczulewicz. So my name there is Lewis, Patrick Lewis. But here, please call me Szczulewicz.”

“All right, Mr. Szczulewicz. And what is your brother's name?”

“Also Szczulewicz. Isaac Szczulewicz, from Warsaw.”

“But he could have changed his name, too, Mr. Szczulewicz, though not because of a pronunciation problem.”

“That's a fine thing!”

“First, you'll have to shave off your mustache. Then announce in the paper that you are looking for your brother.”

“Without my mustache, my wife won't recognize me.”

“But your brother might.”

“Warsaw is all different.”

“The Germans destroyed it.”

“I know, I heard, but I didn't believe it.”

“A few days in Warsaw, and you'll start believing all kinds of things. Take me, for example. I work a newsstand at the corner of two streets that don't exist. . . . I mean, the numbering and the houses are all different. Through the window of my booth I watch Warsaw and wait for the others."

"The others?"

"You'll see for yourself."

"I'm just passing through. There is too little time . . . But let me invite you to a café. We'll have a chat. You're also from Warsaw?"

"I was born on Pawia Street, Number Four, on the sixth floor."

"And I on Gęsia Street. That makes us neighbors."

There were few customers at the café at that hour. We sat by the window.

"I'm always comparing people to other people, particularly to those who are no more. I can't help it," I said, and scrutinized Patrick Lewis a.k.a. Pincus Szczulewicz. "But I'm not sure who you look like."

"I have the same problem. On the plane I sat next to a lady who looked like my aunt Pesa Nachman. She even had the same hairstyle."

"But some people do come back. That's why I wait. For them. When I applied for my job, the manager said: 'Take another kiosk, one in a busier spot. You'll make more and have a better class of people.' But I said: 'No, Mr. Manager, this is the kiosk I want.' And Chaya Sklepik did return. She went through the worst. Now she roams the streets and doesn't recognize anyone. . . ."

"What did she go through?"

"She had spirit, that girl . . . One day she snuck out of the Ghetto through a hole in the wall, to the Aryan side. Came back, that evening, with a bag of bread, which she distributed among the poor on Wołyńska Street."

"You mean one couldn't leave the Ghetto?"

"You don't know anything! For leaving the Ghetto, Mr. Lewis-Szczulewicz, and being found on an Aryan street, you were shot. Chaya went out several times. And she looked as Jewish as you can look. Dark . . ."

"Spaniards and Italians are dark, too."

"You should have told that to Hitler, Mr. Lewis-Szczulewicz. I agree with you. Generalissimo Franco, for example, looks like Solomon Weitzer, the porter on Gęsia Street, but that didn't help Solomon Weitzer."

"What happened to him?"

"He was trying to pull his sister Dora from the train, when a German bastard came up and said: 'It's you or her.' So he got into the car, and she stayed behind."

"I don't understand. Why wouldn't he let his sister take the train out of Warsaw? And what did the German have to do with it?"

"I forgot that you're from Haiti. . . . God Almighty, look what it's come to, Jew cannot understand Jew. Mr. Lewis-Szczulewicz, you travel first-class, in your upholstered seat you read the paper and have a brandy. Here during the Occupation things were a little different. Dora Weitzer was a beautiful girl, I was in love with her, and so was everybody else. . . . Tall, slender . . . Anyway, she didn't want to leave Warsaw. But Jews were made to leave, by the thousands. They were hunted, delivered to the *Umschlagsplatz,* loaded into cattle cars, pushed, packed in by force . . ."

"I see."

"What do you see?"

"Solomon Weitzer was a hero. He gave his life to save his sister."

"Hero! What do you know of it? Fathers and mothers saved their children the same way, thousands of them. . . . Thousands of heroes and heroines! They died with the thought that they had saved their children, but a few days later the children went into the furnace, too. There was a woman, her name was Tolla Mintzowa, she was the physician and director of the Jewish Orphanage at Międzyszyn near Warsaw. But in nineteen forty-two, in August, she went to the gas chamber with her little son, Karol, and all her charges, two hundred Jewish orphans. She was offered a chance to escape, there was even a hideout prepared for her, but she refused. . . ."

"And at Międzyszyn. My God, I used to take a cottage there, a summer place. . . . My God!"

"Why did you come to Warsaw, Mr. Lewis or Szczulewicz? Here I've depressed you, and tonight you may have bad dreams. . . ."

We made an appointment for the following day. About two o'clock there was a knock at the door of the kiosk. It was a stranger. "Hello," he said. "I'm Szczulewicz, remember? I shaved it off."

"Wait a moment!" I said. "I know who you look like. On our street there was a man named Isaac Kopyto. The spit and image of you. Isaac Kopyto! Heavy, tough . . . He was a porter at the Centos."

"I bet that's my brother. The first name is right."

"I don't know. Maybe. Kopyto wasn't his real name."

"What, did he do something bad?"

"No, but Dora Weitzer and he . . ."

"Go on."

"Nothing. I advise you to call the Red Cross and the Jewish Committee. Maybe they can tell you something about Isaac Kopyto. It's your business . . ."

I slammed the door of the kiosk, locked it, and hung the CLOSED sign in the window. I sat there until late at night.

A few days later, that Patrick-Pincus character knocked at the window and said, "I have news for you." And he told me about the meeting with his brother.

"Following your advice, I went to the Jewish Committee. After an hour I found out from those good people my brother's address. I went there and found him at home with his wife and little daughter. They received me cordially, gave me tea, some sort of wafer things to eat, and then my brother and I went to another room, and this is what he told me: 'Pincus, I have to ask you to leave us in peace. I can't have anything to do with you. You're a capitalist, I'm a Communist. In my dossier in the personnel office where I work I wrote that I had no relatives abroad, and that's how I want it to remain.' Those were the words of my brother, Isaac Szczulewicz. What do you make of that? Apparently, I don't have a brother anymore. . . . What a strange country, what strange people. And his wife's name, by the way, was Dora."

That was two years ago. I still work the newsstand and keep seeing Chaya Sklepik in her color-changing kerchief and the man who looks like Mendel Bir. But no Dora Weitzer.

Missing Pieces

I'm not typical. I saw no Nazis, SS-men, or Gestapo, I never laid eyes on a German soldier, and never heard a bomb or a mine explode. I learned of all this after my return. Yes . . . I spent the entire war at my brother Isaac's in New York City. Nobody in my family perished, nobody was gassed, nobody was shot in the forest or starved to death in the Ghetto. As a Warsaw Jew, I'm an exception, and to tell you the truth, it's embarrassing. I wrote a long letter to my brother, telling him about all the horrors I heard. I waited six months for a reply. Finally he sent me a postcard from some scenic place in Florida, with this message: "Don't dig up the War, you'll make yourself sick. You suffer from indigestion as it is. Remember how you caught pneumonia when you were with us? So take care of yourself. Greetings from my Hannah and from Aunt Luba. Your brother."

After a long search I found myself a wife who also had not been in the Ghetto, who had spent no time in a camp, and had not lived through the Occupation in the forest. She was in Uzbekistan the whole time—in Samarkand and later Tashkent. She returned from the east and I from the west, but we're compatible.

My wife, Rose, speaks a little Russian and Uzbek, while I know a little English. She cooks rice dishes, even the desserts have rice in them, while I remember the hamburgers and the pizza I had in a bar on Twelfth Street.

Anyway, I said to my Rose: "Listen, dear, I can't stand being an exception, I want to be like everyone else. People look at me as if I were abnormal, or they think I'm lying."

"You're an honest man," said Rose, "but a little absent-minded. You don't even remember your shoe size."

"That's not what I mean, dear," I explained. "I, Gabriel Lewin, need a new curriculum vitae."

"You have a fine curriculum vitae," she protested. "Any Jew would be proud to have such a curriculum vitae. Who else spent the War in Manhattan, U.S.A.? Who else, in nineteen forty-three, strolled peacefully down Fifth Avenue or Broadway, and ate in kosher restaurants, and had matzo on Pesach? Who else in Warsaw managed that? Nobody else!"

"People don't believe me," I said. "And I can't blame them."

"Maybe they're jealous."

"Maybe, maybe not. In any case, it's hard to live with."

So Rose took some blank sheets of paper out of a sideboard drawer, and we got to work. It was a complicated job. She decided to redo her curriculum vitae, too. Every evening we sat at the table and put together our life histories during the Occupation.

We began with September, 1939. Although Rose was not in Warsaw then, she recalled several radio bulletins from that period, and conversations about the War, in the village of Nowojelnia where she lived with her parents. We constructed two pages of my curriculum vitae out of this. I learned how long the Nazi air raids lasted, what was bombed and where, and that on September 7, Major Umiastowski over the radio asked all male inhabitants to leave the city. In my new curriculum vitae, I stayed in the capital, and from September 7 to September 20 (Rose didn't remember the exact date—toward the end of the month, in any case) bombs fell on my street: high-explosive, incendiary, delayed action, and some that, because of sabotage back in German factories, did not go off but lay peacefully in the middle of the street.

Before I went to America, I lived at Przebieg Street No. 2 on the fifth floor, and from our window you could see into a room on the fourth floor of the house across the street. My grandmother told me that Mr. and Mrs. Jung lived there, and that their daughter had emigrated to America and was not called Jung anymore, but Young with a Y and an O. Miss Young made a great career for herself there; she got a part in a film, then a Hollywood contract, and became a star. I wasn't sure if this was true or not, but I added a passage to my curriculum vitae about going down to the air-raid shelter with the Jungs and their telling me about their daughter, the great actress Loretta Young with a Y and an O. Such details add realism. Rose approved of the idea.

A description of the Germans' entry into Warsaw I found in some library books. The trouble started in 1940. Reading, we filled ourselves with so many atrocities that we couldn't eat, drink, sleep, or think like normal people anymore. This went on for days.

One sleepless night, Rose sat up in bed and said: "Gabriel,

according to my new curriculum vitae, I couldn't have survived. I must have died of a heart attack. Because I can't stand the sight of blood. I used to run away when the *shochet* came to kill the chickens and ducks, I cried when I cut my finger. I could never have lived through those horrors of nineteen forty, and we have three more years to go, nineteen forty-one, nineteen forty-two, and nineteen forty-three."

"If all Jews were like you, dear wife," I said, "the whole Ghetto would have dropped dead, and the Nazis wouldn't have had anything to do. I, on the other hand, have enlisted in the Jewish partisan army and am now in the forest, fighting the Germans as becomes a young man of courage."

"Nobody enlisted to join the partisans," Rose explained to me, her brother having been with the underground in the Polesie region. "You had to get yourself detailed to it by order, and that wasn't so easy."

I deleted the part of my curriculum vitae which described me as an underground soldier, and put myself in occupied Warsaw again, but outside the Ghetto, on the Aryan side, where I lived with the Wieczorek brothers on Marimoncka Street, under the identity of a relative of theirs who had been expelled from Nazi-annexed Poznań. The old Wieczorek couple were well-known to my parents and grandparents. We used to play hide-and-seek with Wacek and Adam near the Citadel, and when we were bigger, it was Indians, and when we were bigger still, we went on long walks along the Vistula toward Młociny.

My curriculum vitae was coming along nicely. Rose also added to hers a few "gallant adventures," as she called them, and so after a few weeks we got to the year 1943.

"No, there is no way we could have lived through that,"

said Rose, and burst into tears. "Don't ask me to survive the destruction of the Białystok ghetto. And I won't have you suffer in the one in Warsaw."

"Why Białystok?" I asked her.

"Because I wrote that I escaped to Białystok, to my uncle Oscar Weisberg," she said.

We were sitting at breakfast. I pushed my plate away, set the glass of milk aside, and looked at Rose. She was crying: her eyes were closed tight, but tears were running, one after the other, down her wrinkled cheeks.

"Don't cry, silly!" I said loudly, perhaps a little too loudly, to cover my pity for her.

"I am crying out of grief, but also with a tiny gladness," she sobbed. "Grief for my family and the loss of so many innocent people, yet I can't help being happy that I wasn't in a camp, in a ghetto, in the forest, or some other place where they murdered children, since I was a child then."

"Nineteen years old is not a child," I said. "There were babies, toddlers there. Like our neighbor's Marylka. She was only three, and you can imagine . . ." I got up and went to the window. In the sandbox down in the yard, children were playing—squealing, laughing, skipping, rolling in the sand. A boy in red pants and white shirt was crying, while another boy, a little taller, patted his little ginger-haired head. A girl in a green dress was reading a book, bent over so that one couldn't see her face. Beside her stood a boy holding a transistor radio to his ear. I asked my wife to come to the window and said:

"Imagine that suddenly, from behind the house on the corner, and from behind the garage and the shed, step German soldiers, field police, SS-men, and they surround the sandbox. The children go on playing, not seeing them or sensing the danger. At last the boy with the radio notices the Germans and screams. He throws the radio to the ground and tries to flee. The girl runs after him, clutching her book, and a few other children run. But it is too late. . . . The SS-men form the children into a double column and march them to the street, where trucks have pulled up. The children are off to the ovens. And there among them is Marylka, who has knocked at our door every day and said, 'Good morning, Auntie. Good morning, Uncle.' Now she won't knock at our door anymore."

Silently we stood together at the window. Then we went back to the table.

"I know a woman who has only the second half of her curriculum vitae," mused Rose. "The first half got away from her, and she can't find it."

"You mean Janeczka?" I asked.

"Yes," she said. "I was thinking of Janeczka."

We had met Janeczka in a dairy bar. We used to drop in there for blintzes. She worked in the kitchen, but later became the cashier. She always greeted us with a smile. She had big black eyes, long eyelashes, and tawny skin. The other girls called her Gypsy. One summer day we saw her near the Old Watchtower, sitting against a wall. She beckoned to us. When we went up to her, she said, "I sprained my foot and can't walk. Could you help me?"

I flagged a taxi, and we took her to a first-aid station and then to her place. We became friends. She visited us; we visited her. Then, during one of our evening conversations, she told us:

"I don't know who I am. I don't know who my mother was

or my father. Mrs. Eliza, who took me from a children's shelter in nineteen thirty-eight or nineteen thirty-nine, died on Freta Street during the Warsaw Uprising. I was wounded in the foot by shrapnel—the same foot I sprained at the Watchtower that time. A gentleman and a beautiful lady took me under their wing. Her name was Teresa Anna. I wasn't with them very long. I ended up in the orphanage.

"I'm searching for my parents, for the house in which I was born. If the house is gone, the street must surely be there, the lot, or something. I walk all over Warsaw, checking, one after another, the prewar streets, in Praga, in Wola, in Ochota, in Mokotów. I know I'll find that street.

"When I close my eyes, I see a dark room and two beds. I see the face of a young woman in a gray beret, and there is a necklace of little red corals around her throat. I've seen this for years. I remember three gaslights in the street, but nothing more. Sometimes I have doubts, I wonder if maybe I made up those pictures from my childhood. My childhood is like the missing piece of a puzzle—a small piece, but so important."

Rose went back to the window. She opened it wide, and you could hear the mingled sound of laughter, talk, and the shouts of children playing.

"How good it is that it's day, that it's warm, and that children are playing in the sandbox," said my wise wife.

And just then it occurred to me that Janeczka's eyes were exactly like those of my little cousin Esther in Scarsdale, New York.

Five Mouths to Feed

"Here's a skinned rabbit and three pigeons. What do I get?"

The old man touched the rabbit with a finger. "This one, maybe, was dead. Maybe you pulled it out of the garbage."

I was insulted. "I don't do such things. My goods are fresh. The pigeons are young, they may not have much meat on them, but they'll be better for you than old fruit peels and ground chestnuts. Pay me fair, old-timer, and tomorrow I'll see what I can do in the way of horsemeat and potatoes."

The old man inspected the rabbit, then shoved it into his bag.

"It isn't much," he said, "for all our hungry stomachs. Make an effort, son, to get us better meat. Fish, perhaps. I haven't had fish in a long while. And a little liquor. I'll pay you." He fished two squashed gray cigarettes from his pocket and gave me one.

I lit it, drew on it, inhaled. The smoke was acrid and made me choke. I wondered how the old man would pay.

"Rats everywhere," he said. "But I draw the line there. I

won't eat them. They squeak and squeak, all night. Today you get a wedding band, so you'll have to throw in something else."

I agreed and took four big sugar beets from my haversack.

The old man grimaced. "Not enough."

I tossed in the last two and said, "Tomorrow I'll bring the horsemeat. There'll be several kilos of it."

The ring was gold and had two letters inside, A and R, and a date, 6/7/1900.

"Whose is it?" I asked.

"I don't ask you how you got the rabbit," he said. "Don't ask me how I got the ring. Your rabbit is damned expensive."

"Everything's expensive," I said.

The old man squinted at me. "You think maybe I have a treasure chest, a pile of gold? Bring that horsemeat. I'll give you a ruby. A real ruby."

"Tell me, old-timer," I asked, "do you have any hope?"

He reflected. "Hope? A stupid question. You skin me alive and ask me if I have hope." He fell silent, then said at last, "I want to live until we're free, and for that I'll eat shit if I have to. I'd like a bath, too, but that would cost another wedding ring, wouldn't it? These rings come from dead hands. The bodies are over there, in the sewers. We escaped. We're always escaping, running, hiding in the ground. Look at me, I'm like a mole. Black snout, hands like spades. There are several of us, all black, all starving. They're waiting for this carrion. It will hold them for a few hours. They know you bring it, but they also know you could turn us in anytime. When the rings run out, maybe you will come with Germans."

"Old and stupid, that's what you are," I said, angry. "I trade in meat and beets, not people. I'm looking out for myself. When the War ends, I'll have gold in my pocket. Before the War I ate potatoes and potatoes, after the War I'll have pastry and oranges. It's that simple."

"You're right," he said. "You're like me. I want to live, and you want to live, and nothing else counts. Remember, tomorrow at the same time. I'll be waiting. You'll get the ruby."

"I'll be there," I said.

When I returned to our cellar, America was sitting on a barrel, smoking a cigar. On another barrel stood a burning carbide lamp.

"Where did you get the cigar?" I asked.

"Found it," she said. "Four boxes in a cellar nearby. And you, who did you trade with?"

"The same lot as yesterday and the day before, and last week."

"They gave you something?"

"Yes."

"Throw it away," she said.

"America, what are you talking about?"

"Throw it away or return it. I've thought this over."

I took the wedding band from my pocket and held it on my palm. "Look," I said quietly, "look at it."

"Get rid of it," she ordered.

"I won't throw it away, but I'll give them pork tomorrow, free. All right?"

"And the next day."

"And the next day."

She got up, paced, sat down again. "How many of them are there?" she asked.

"I don't know," I replied. "Five or six, I think."

"Children?"

"I'm not sure."

"We're going back to New York." She jumped off the barrel. "Here, I found two silver candlesticks, put them in the sack. And a mortar and pestle."

I stowed the candlesticks and the mortar and pestle in our bags. Then we crossed to Ogrodowa Street by the sewer and surfaced. It was dark outside, drizzling.

"The night will be over before long," whispered America. "Hurry up."

We ran past ruined tenements, then turned into a garden. America stopped. I stopped, too, and immediately heard jabbering in German. We crouched down. The policemen were coming from the other direction.

"Don't be afraid," she whispered.

"Who's afraid?" I whispered back, but I was always afraid of the Germans.

The policemen stopped. One of them sneezed and blew his nose.

"Has a cold," America whispered with a smile.

The policemen stood there a while, then turned back. We ran toward a little summerhouse, passed it, and through a hole in a fence entered a courtyard. A feeble light burned in the porter's lodge, visible through a badly drawn curtain.

"It's already five," America said. "The porter gets up at five."

The stairs creaked under us, and then we were in New York. America started a fire in the range, while I unloaded the sacks, put the items on the floor, and wiped them clean with a rag.

"The candlesticks are beautiful," I said, "but the mortar is garbage."

"Put it on the chest, and the candlesticks behind the bed. The rest can go under the bed." She took two plates out of the sideboard and set them on the table. "Sit. The soup will be ready in a minute."

I studied America as she salted the soup, straightened the burners with the poker, poured water into the teapot, and took half a loaf of bread from the cupboard. "How old are you?" I asked.

She stopped what she was doing and turned around. "How old I am doesn't matter. I'm not your mother, I'm not your wife, I'm your partner and nothing more. Understand?"

I nodded.

She came closer. "And get this through your head. You don't go into town by yourself. We go together. After the War you can do what you like, but for now . . ."

"You need me," I said.

She slapped my face. "What was that, you bastard?" she whispered.

"I need you," I answered.

"We need each other," she said, and went back to the range.

America had pulled me out of the rubble. I had been going through cellars after a German raid, when suddenly something crashed overhead and I found myself in darkness. Then a plank hit me, and that was all I remembered. I had heard about her. She prowled the rubble fields with a little mongrel called Diamond. Diamond would warn her of Germans approaching by a barely audible yip. The dog had also got buried under rubble just then, and it was during her search for him that she found me. Diamond was never seen again—either the Germans shot him or he was crushed beneath falling masonry.

"I used to work in a nightclub," said America, taking her place at the table. "People thought I was ten years younger than I was. That was unusual, because girls wear out fast in that line of work, but I didn't. I knew how to draw the line. Then I married an American."

"Where is he now?"

"Who knows?"

We ate in silence, slowly. I saw that she had something on her mind. At last she said in her husky voice, "We have to help those sewer people. Move them to a decent place."

"There goes our business with them." But I knew she was right: they couldn't stay where they were.

"Don't be stupid! They'll pay for their food, the moving, and the good deed all in one. A lump sum!"

"But didn't you tell me to throw the wedding ring away?"

"You were taking advantage."

"I'm adding pork cuts."

"Good."

"And where will we move them?" I asked.

"I have an idea."

"As long as there's gold in it."

"You *are* a bastard." America smiled. "Hand over the bottle, we'll drink to success."

I took the bottle of homemade liquor out of the sideboard. The stuff upset my stomach, but I never let on. I poured myself half a glass, but America downed a whole one, poured another, and drank that, too.

"Now I'll show you how I used to dance the tango with my American," she said.

She got up, pulled off her sweater, her pants, and put on a long dirty dress she had scavenged somewhere, and earrings, and a gold bracelet on each wrist. She tied a green scarf around her neck, powdered her nose, and put on lipstick.

"Now I'm ready!" she said. "Sing! Sing 'Tango Milonga'!"

We both sang, and America danced. She danced around the table, around me, around the chairs, tilting her head coquettishly, her eyes half-closed. I had never seen her dance before. I noticed, for the first time, a long scar behind her right ear.

Dancing, whirling faster and faster, crooning to herself, she took my hand and made me dance with her. But the floor began rising and falling, and the homemade liquor rushed up to my gorge. Before I passed out, I vomited all over America's dress.

She returned toward evening, bringing pork cuts, two loaves of bread, and small pieces of soap.

"You almost got me in the face with your puke," she said, laughing.

I mumbled an apology. "I just can't drink."

"Let's go see those people. Are you up to it?"

"The sewer people?"

"Yes."

"And where are you taking them?"

"I found a place. You know where the sand digger started a house on the riverbank? He didn't finish the building, only the foundations. The basement caved in years ago and is overgrown, but there's a concealed entrance to it from the bank."

"It's haunted," I said. "It was haunted before the War. The sand digger hanged himself in that basement, because his wife ran away. She ran away right after the wedding. They say his ghost is there."

"Germans are worse than a ghost. If the sewer people can live with the rats, they won't mind the departed sand digger."

"What are we making on this deal?"

"I don't know. Dress warmly, the night is cold and the way is long."

I got out of bed, splashed cold water on my face, and drank a large mug of tea. I put on two pairs of pants, two shirts, a sweater, a vest, and an oversize jacket with big pockets, into which I put my tools: a hammer, pliers, a crowbar, candles, matches, string, and a pocketknife. I also wore a cap with earflaps. America was dressed much the same, but had first-rate parachutist boots on her feet, while mine were only rubber. We each carried a haversack containing a rolled-up sleeping bag and a hunk of bread wrapped in paper.

We snuck out just before the curfew and reached the sewer without incident. America was first to go down the manhole. We couldn't see, but we knew the way. I didn't light a candle until Rymarska Street. It was nine o'clock, by America's watch, when we surfaced. I left her in the cellar of a gutted house and ran by the route I knew among the ruins, squeezed through a hole in a wall, and found myself at the meeting place. The old man crept out from behind a pile of bricks and took a seat on the ground.

"I don't have the food," I said, "I have a proposition."

The old man was silent.

"I have a proposition," I repeated.

"So what is it?" he finally asked.

"We want to move you to a better place."

"Who's we, and why?"

"Myself and my partner, America. That's what they call her."

"And for this, I pay?"

"Yes."

"And you don't get paid by the Gestapo or the gendarmes?"

"I don't trade in people."

"What guarantee do I have?"

"Guarantee?"

"Without a guarantee, we're not going. Don't come anymore."

"Wait," I said, angry. "I'll be back. Let me talk to my partner."

I went back to America.

"I knew you wouldn't be able to handle it," she said. "I'll talk to them myself."

The old man was still sitting on the ground. The sky had cleared a little, and you could see his face. He had a long white beard, a broad nose, and one eye covered with black tape. He wore a cap with a visor. America sat down beside him.

"You pay a little now, the rest after the War," she said. "Hide the money in the ground somewhere, conceal it carefully."

"I don't know you."

"I could have brought the gendarmes here, you know, and

not had to argue." America got up. "If you don't like the idea, don't do it. Go somewhere else. We have to stop bringing food here, though."

The old man thought it over, then rose and said: "I'll ask my people. Wait. It may take a while. Give me an hour."

I yelled at her for postponing the payment. "Who knows when the War will end, or whether the old man will make it, or even whether he has the money?"

"You can have my gold bracelets," she said.

That I hadn't expected. The bracelets were thin, one engraved with delicate little roses, the other with daisies. America knew I wanted them because I had offered to swap three rings and a pair of earrings for them. But she wouldn't hear of it then.

When the old man appeared with his flock, my first reaction was that they were evil spirits. Dark figures of various sizes stood in a row before us, five of them, including the old man. They didn't speak. America went out through the hole in the wall, and they followed her. I brought up the rear, feeling depressed somehow, as if I was in for a lot of trouble.

We walked through the sewers slowly and in silence. The water at times reached to our waists. The old man took one child in his arms; America and I took turns carrying another. Once or twice we halted to rest. At last we crawled out onto a dark street which led to the embankment. We met nobody along the way, only cats, who hunted in the stinking piles of garbage. The stink kept away the Germans; they rarely ventured into this neighborhood. America had chosen the hideout well.

In the sand digger's cellar it was dry, though full of rubbish. You could hear the river flowing nearby, and the trains clanging across the bridge.

It was raining heavily outside.

"The rain protects us," the old man said. "It washes away our footprints, drives off the rats and our enemies. May it rain, rain for days and nights. Look, see the rain . . ." he said to his children and grandchildren.

"Tomorrow we'll bring food," said America. "Barricade yourselves in with planks and rocks. Go out only at night. Bury your shit. You'll need fresh water, too."

"What about the payment?" I asked when we got back to New York.

"They have nothing," she said, pulling off her boots.

"I don't believe it."

"The old man gave you his last wedding ring yesterday, and the ruby he lied about. He told me when we were in the sewer."

"He's lying now!" I shouted, close to tears.

"No, I believe him."

"And what now?"

"I told you. You get the bracelets. You don't lose."

And she took them out of their secret compartment in the wall and handed them over. I quickly slipped them into my pocket.

Next morning, America went out before noon, saying that she was going into the countryside for pork cuts. I waited two days. I looked for her in town, I asked the sewer people, I checked the railroad station and the market, but without success. Nobody had seen her. Left by myself, I could have moved to the country and stayed with a farmer I knew, but now I had the old man and his family on my back.

I have five mouths to feed. It won't be easy. I've used all the wedding rings and gold chains. All I have left are the two bracelets, but those I'm saving for my cousin Halinka, and the end of the War is not in sight.

I keep waiting for my partner, although last week I heard from several people that the gendarme we call "Boozy" shot her at the garbage dump near the river, where the cats prowl for rats and the rats for cadavers. Where the stink is worst. I looked there, once, on my way back from the sewer people, but found no trace of America.

Editor's Note

The stories in this collection were taken from the following of Stanislaw Benski's books:

So Much Fire Around (*Tyle ognia wokoło,* Krajowa agencja wydawnicza, Warsaw, 1979): Trouble Sleeping (Krótki sen), Five Mouths to Feed (Pięć wygłodzonych gąb)

The Most Important Part (*Ta najważniejsza cząsteczka,* Czytelnik, Warsaw, 1982): The Round (Wielki obchód), The Tzaddik's Grandson (Prawnuczek cadyka), Colored Drawings (Kolorowe rysunki), The Viper (Żmija), Diamond or Glass (Brylanty i szkiełka), On the Corner (Dwie ulice i kozie różki), Forty-nine Visits (Sto czterdziesty trzeci dzień), Syndrome (Pierwszy i ostatni klient), Missing Pieces (Ta najważniejsza cząsteczka), Snapshot (Cztery fotografie)

The Emperor's Waltz (*Cesarski walc,* Wydawnictwo literackie, Kraków, 1985): Sulamith (Sulamit), A Phone Call from London (Telefon z Londynu)

The Survivors (*Ocaleni,* Czytelnik, Warsaw, 1986): Three Left (excerpts from the novel)

Guardian of the Holidays (*Strażnik świąt,* Wydawnictwo literackie, Kraków, 1987): A Strange Country (Dziwny kraj i dziwni ludzie)

Franklin Pierce College Library
00016583
APR 20 2007
Printed in USA